THE BLACK TERROR

Troubled man Martin Clegg has always suffered from dreams which seem intensely real. In them, bizarrely, he's another person — not of this Earth! He's finally forced to confide in his fiancée, Elsie Barlow, and they consult Martin's scientifically inclined friend Tom Cavendish. He reveals, astonishingly, that Martin has a cosmic twin to whom he's mentally linked. Unsuspecting, they are about to become caught up in the strands of an incredible cosmic mystery that will, inexorably, be played out . . .

JOHN RUSSELL FEARN

---- ◆ ----

THE
BLACK TERROR

Complete and Unabridged

LINFORD
Leicester

First published in Great Britain

First Linford Edition
published 2010

British Library CIP Data

Fearn, John Russell, *1908 – 1960.*
  The black terror. – –
  (Linford mystery library)
  1. Science fiction.
  2. Large type books.
  I. Title II. Series
  823.9'12–dc22

  ISBN 978–1–44480–495–9

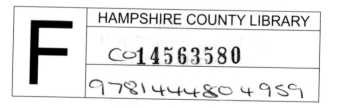
This book is printed on acid-free paper

1

Cosmic Twin

Martin Clegg had always been aware of it since he had first taken a conscious interest in life. It was a vague something, as indeterminate as a nebula, only assuming a degree of reality during the hours when he slept. Somewhere he had a twin, if not in body then in thought — and as he grew older it became an increasingly disturbing factor in his life. It was not easy to almost live two lives and not make a good job of either of them.

Outwardly, Martin Clegg was similar to any young man of twenty-five. He had the three inseparable adjuncts of his age — a job, good health, and a girlfriend. He spent his days as a draughtsman, his evenings with Elsie Barlow, and his nights with — He didn't know what. Something. That Other, that mystical conscious being who was half himself and half somebody else. Far away, yet becoming increasingly dominating.

In appearance Martin was not particularly fascinating. He had no looks to speak of, his main virtue being a ruggedly chiselled face, which made him appear many years older than he was. His hair was black and untidy; his eyes a piercing grey. Those with an understanding of human nature would have said he probably could be clever but was too apt to wander from the main point ever to bring anything to a successful conclusion. There was a reason for this, though — That Something, that Other. Far, far away.

Elsie Barlow noticed the increasing dreaminess of Martin and did not particularly like it. Being a completely natural girl with an everyday outlook on life, a girl who punched a keyboard by day and spent her evenings thinking of the future with Martin, she found it disturbing when he cultivated the habit of walking like a somnambulist and only answering her questions when she neatly underlined them with a nudge in the ribs.

'Mart, what on earth is the *matter* with you?' she demanded one evening, and halted their slow walk past brilliantly lighted shop windows.

It was the week before Christmas and they had decided to take a 'viewing' expedition to determine what they should buy for their relatives and friends. Only Mart's interest was plainly miles away. His face was thoughtful, his eyes looking through Elsie as she questioned him.

'Am I talking to myself?' she enquired.

Martin still looked at her. He hardly noticed her face, rosy cheeked from the icy wind, or the curls of fair hair peeping from under her saucy little hat. He was looking into an abyss where there was a powdering of brilliant stars and, amidst them, Something calling. Something irresistible —

'*Mart!*'

Elsie's voice knifed through Martin's consciousness and he gave a start. She was there in front of him, her hands on her hips and profound exasperation on her pretty face. Men and women, muffled against the wind, were going back and

3

forth in the bright lights. 'Remember me?' Elsie asked sourly. 'I'm the girl who came out with you on a shopping tour. You might as well be a corpse.'

'There may be more in that than you realize,' Martin replied, thinking.

'What?' Then Elsie caught impulsively at his arm. 'Mart, what's wrong? Why do you behave so strangely these days? Are you ill, or something?'

'No, I'm not ill. Never felt better — physically.'

'Then what is it? After all, I am your fiancée. If you can't tell me, there's nobody else.'

'I don't think you'd believe me if I did tell you.'

Elsie hesitated, momentarily unsure of him. Then she said brightly: 'No harm in trying, is there? At least let me know what it's all about.'

'Very well. Come with me.'

Martin took her arm and to her surprise he led her away from the bright lights of the street and down numerous back alleyways. Though she had known him for many months now, and he had always treated her with quiet gentility, she did begin to wonder if perhaps something had changed him — if he was perhaps an unsuspected psychopath and might murder her. His grip on her arm was certainly fierce. She thought of making a dash for it, but just at that moment they came out on to the open expanse of Ridley's Common — a great, barren area of dry grass and clods of earth supposed to be a recreational centre. Actually it was one of those bare spots inseparable from any provincial town.

'Nice and dark here,' Mart said, lowering his hand.

'Yes.' Elsie laughed uneasily. 'Isn't it?'

'What's the matter?' Mart sounded mildly surprised. 'You sound scared!'

'I — I hardly know how I sound, Mart. You're acting so strangely . . . '

He looked at her in the starlight. Out here in this empty expanse the lights of the city were dimmed and instead the sky was the only illumination, frostily bright in the cold air.

'Good heavens, Elsie, you didn't think I was going to murder you or something, did you?' Mart laughed incredulously for a moment and then drew the girl to him and held her tightly. 'Dammit, you're even trembling,' he added. 'It's all my fault for being so morose . . . I wouldn't hurt you for all the gold in the world, sweetheart. I love you too much — '

He became practical again as he released her. 'My only reason for coming here is so that we can see the sky clearly. I hope it may help my explanation.'

'Oh?' Elsie was at ease again now, her arm about his waist. She surveyed the star-dusted emptiness overhead, then waited.

'Up there,' Martin said, pointing, 'is the constellation of Orion. See it?'

'I — I think so, Mart. I'm not very good at astronomy.'

'I mean that cluster — *there*. That's Orion. You can faintly see the double-star Rigel, ruddy Betelgeuse, and beyond is Aldebaran — that red one.'

'Well?' Elsie asked curiously. 'What about it?'

'This will sound crazy,' Mart said, his voice quiet, 'but I have the feeling that I belong up there.'

'Crazy is right! Oh, for heaven's sake, Mart, what in the world are you talking about? Do you mean you've dragged me all this way just to talk nonsense?'

'It isn't nonsense, Elsie. I was never more dead serious in my life!'

'But — but — ' Elsie made a bewildered movement. 'How can you belong up there? I know you like astronomy — you've mentioned it enough times — but you don't have to let it go to your head like this, do you?'

'It goes back a long way,' Mart said, in the same brooding tone. 'Ever since I was about six years old and first started to take a conscious interest in things. I have never in all my life had a decent night's sleep, because the moment I am asleep I seem to be somebody else. It isn't frustration, the repression of daytime desires, or anything like that. I — I have a twin somewhere, and I believe he's up there.'

Elsie was silent. To have to wrestle with a problem like this was almost beyond her.

7

'Have — have you seen a psychiatrist?' she asked. 'He could probably make you straight.'

Martin turned slightly, surprised. 'Matter of fact, no. I never thought of it. I just accepted the phenomenon and let it go at that. Lately it has become much worse. I feel this other self pushing its way into my own personality with a sense of urgency — or something.'

'It's time you did something about it,' Elsie said. 'It really is. Why not act immediately? Sir Robert Cranwell has his rooms in town and lives on the premises. He'd perhaps make an exception and see you tonight, just as a doctor would . . . You're so utterly changed, Mart. You owe it to me, if not to yourself, to find out what ails you.'

As Martin hesitated he found his arm seized and, almost in spite of himself, Elsie began drawing him away. She did not release her grip until they had returned to the brightly lighted main street and had the door of Sir Robert Cranwell's residence before them. Elsie thumbed the bell over the shining brass plate.

The psychiatrist was at home, it appeared, but Elsie had to talk very convincingly to the maid before she succeeded in getting the required interview. Sir Robert rose from the chair in his consulting room as the two were shown into him. He was a tall, eagle-like man with white hair brushed back firmly from a high forehead.

'This is very gracious of you, Sir Robert,' Elsie said, as she shook hands. 'Only extreme urgency would have made me so insistent — Er — it concerns my fiancé, here — Martin Clegg.'

'I am always ready to help if I can,' Sir Robert smiled. 'What seems to be the trouble, Mr. Clegg?'

'I have a kinship with somebody or something in the constellation of Orion,' Martin answered deliberately, and this made the psychiatrist clear his throat.

'Ah — I see — Hmm . . . Extraordinary. Suppose we go into it more fully, eh? You, Miss Barlow, will find the ante-room comfortable, I am sure.'

Patiently, but firmly, Elsie was conducted into the adjoining room and the door was closed. Here she remained — for over an hour. Part of the time she skimmed through periodicals; the rest of the time she paced up and down anxiously — then at last the door opened and Martin reappeared with the psychiatrist behind him. Elsie turned sharply and looked at them. 'Well?' she asked quickly. 'It isn't anything — serious, is it?'

'Great heavens, no!' Sir Robert gave a reassuring smile. 'Mr. Clegg and I have had quite an interesting chat and I think he can be cured with a course of treatment. What he chooses to tell you, Miss Barlow, is his own affair. I, of course, cannot divulge anything any more than can a doctor.'

'No — of course not.'

Elsie felt that at that moment the best thing to do was leave, particularly as Martin had a decidedly baffled look on his face. She linked her arm through his and in a moment or two they were out in the street again.

'Well?' she asked presently, as they walked along. 'What was his verdict?'

'The man's an idiot!' Martin said it

with emphatic assurance. 'He traced the trouble back to some incident in my childhood when a can of pineapple fell on my head. The only person who can explain what is the matter with me is a scientist — not a mind-doctor. Tom Cavendish, for instance. I might just catch him in, too. He's an electronic engineer and has been working late recently, but it's towards ten now so we may stand a chance.'

Elsie raised no objections and Martin had guessed right. Tom Cavendish, a young and rather saturnine being, deserted his supper when his mother informed him of the identity of the visitors. He came into the drawing room where they were waiting and shook hands cordially.

'Sorry to bother you, Tom,' Martin apologized, 'but I couldn't think of anybody else likely to have the solution to a scientific problem.'

'Thanks for the flattery,' Tom smiled. 'What seems to be wrong? Television gone haywire?'

'No — his mind,' Elsie said seriously. 'He has the idea he has a twin up in the

11

stars, or something. I never heard of anything so crazy in my life.'

Tom sat down. He had not smiled at the flippant way in which Elsie had spoken. He looked at Martin intently

'Let's have it, Mart,' he suggested; so Martin related his curious story in detail, just as he had told it to the psychiatrist.

'It isn't impossible,' Tom said at last, thinking.

'What!' Elsie looked at him blankly. 'You actually mean to say there might be something in it?'

'It's a matter of understanding the mind,' Tom explained, hunching intently forward. 'You see, many scientists accept the theory that ether — that unknowable something which lies between planets and suns — is actually mind force. Jeans began it when he postulated the theory that the Universe is really only a gigantic thought and that human beings are transformers who interpret the thought-surround into action.'

Elsie just gazed with her eyes wide open, but Martin was listening intently. He knew Tom too well to discredit a single word he uttered.

'Look at it this way,' Tom continued. 'Around us at this moment are radio waves, from all over the world, each one of them carrying some particular programme. We tune a radio set to whatever programme we desire — and in it comes. Scientific theory has it that human brains are, basically, only similar to radio equipment and that they interpret particular wavelengths of thought which exist in the multiform myriads of waves around us. For that reason some people are geniuses, if their brains happen to be able to interpret the highest octaves of thought. Others are criminals if they only interpret the baser waves. In this vast sea of thought that we call the universal empty space there is every conceivable form of wave — or emotion — that we cannot help but interpret according to the quality of our brains. Our bodies are mere dead clay, operated by the brains we possess. In fact the whole Universe — if I may quote Jeans — is only perhaps one gigantic thought of the mind of a super-mathematician.'

'And — and does that explain what is wrong with Martin?' Elsie asked, her voice faltering in spite of herself.

'It might. In the physical world. Nature sometimes produces her work twice — or even five times over — creating twins or quintuplets respectively. It is believed that between twins, at least, there is nearly always a common mental link. If it can exist on Earth, why cannot it exist across untold light-centuries of space?'

'Because only our world has people on it,' Elsie replied.

Tom Cavendish had known Elsie for some months — as a very nice girl but not particularly brainy. So he just smiled at her, and she did not quite like the way he did it, either.

'Our world, Elsie, is probably one of millions with people on it,' he said. 'Science leans more and more to the theory that our world is not exclusive in possessing thinking beings. In fact we are very probably extremely low in the scale compared to some planets — No, we can accept the belief that life teems on other planets as much as it does here. If,

14

however, there existed on a distant world a being with a brain identical to Martin's, it would receive exactly the same wavelengths of thought, just as two radio receivers, tuned to one station, would receive the same programme. In that case, there would arise the phenomenon of linked brains, such as occurs between twins.'

'Linked?' Elsie frowned and pondered.

'Radio sets receiving the same programme are said to be in 'sympathy'. Two brains receiving identical impulses and thoughts from the ether-sea would also be in 'sympathy' with each other. They would be linked — not physically — but by a mental tie, that mental tie being the obvious one of each brain being able to see the same thing. You must admit that when two people can both see the solution of a problem they can very nearly read each other's minds, so en rapport are they with each other. All that happens between twins is that their twinship gives them practically identical brains, so they remain in each other's spheres of influence. It makes no difference if the twin be at the other end of the Universe because thought knows no barriers . . . So, Martin, I think you *have* got a twin.'

'Out in the constellation of Orion?' Martin asked, his voice incredulous.

'Why not? The reason why you become more convinced of it during the sleeping hours is because in that period your individual will, which forms a barrier, is relaxed and this other mind, in tune with yours, affects you with much greater power.' Tom paused for a moment and then asked, 'Have you ever tried communicating?'

'No. When I'm asleep it's impossible, and when I'm awake I do not feel the influence so strongly. My one conviction is a sense of urgency, even fear — as though somebody is urging me to do something, and I don't know what it is.'

'You must try and find out.' Tom suggested. 'Maybe you will, as time goes on. In the meantime I cannot see how this influence can ever cease until one or the other of you . . . dies.'

Martin looked up sharply. 'You really

believe that is the only way?'

'I do. This double of yours in the constellation Orion must be experiencing the same trouble as you. If he is highly scientific he will know the reason for it: if he is not, he will be utterly bewildered.'

There was a good deal more Martin would have liked to ask. In fact he could have stayed all night and talked to Tom, absorbing his immense scientific knowledge — but Elsie had other ideas. She rose from the chair and said prosaically:

'We're keeping you from your supper, Tom — and I'm sure Mart and I want ours. Thanks for being so helpful.'

'I only hope that I have,' Tom answered seriously. 'If you get no better, Mart, come and see me again. Even if I can't cure you I may be able to give you some comfort.'

'Thanks.' Martin shook hands. 'You're a good friend, old man.'

Out in the street, as she and Martin began to drift homewards, Elsie stated flatly exactly what she thought.

'Scientists are fatheads! Ask them a straightforward question and they come out with all manner of high-sounding words. As if you could have a twin up in the stars there! I never heard of anything so crazy!'

'Sometimes, Elsie,' Martin said wearily, 'I think you have a very tiny mind. You're a decent girl, but you — '

'Tiny mind, did you say?' Elsie came to a stop, her lips pouting in the light of the street lamps.

'You must have, otherwise you'd see that Tom's explanation is the only possible one.'

'I don't know which is the crazier — you or Tom!' Elsie snapped. 'But I *do* know I'm not going to walk around with you and be insulted! What sort of fun do you think I'm having? Going out with a man who looks half asleep and explains it by pointing at the stars? I know lots of other chaps who can give me a good time — and the sooner I tell them so, the better!'

'Elsie — wait a minute — '

Martin made a grab at her arm and missed. He sighed and remained where he was, watching her slender figure heading away under the street lamps, her heels clicking purposefully. When at last she had vanished from view round the corner which led to her home avenue he pressed finger and thumb wearily to his eyes.

'Maybe she's right,' he muttered. 'I can't be much of a pal to walk out with.'

He began moving again, mooching along with hands thrust deep in his overcoat pockets. By the time he had reached his rooms he had come to a decision. He locked the door of his little combined apartment and, quite deliberately, went to the small table and began to write a letter. When he had finished he read it through:

December 21st.
To Whom It May Concern,

I, Martin Clegg, have decided for various reasons to take my own life, and I absolutely absolve anybody else from possible blame. I find my life purposeless — and rendered more so by the attitude of my former fiancée, Elsie Barlow, though I can easily understand — and forgive — her impressions of me. I also feel that by dying I may release another person, far away, from the same chains that are holding me. One man may understand — Tom Cavendish. In any case the world will not miss a not-too-good draughtsman.

Martin Clegg.

Martin nodded to himself, put the letter in an envelope and then addressed it to his landlady. This done he crossed to the cupboard and took from it the bottle of sleeping tablets which, his nights always being disturbed, he had taken to using for some months past.

He shook several into his palm, considered, and added several more. Without even troubling to remove his coat or shoes he put the tablets on his tongue, washed them down with water, and then lay on the bed.

He smiled a little as he yawned and drowsiness began to assail him. Though the single light in the room was still on he could see fairly well through the un-curtained window. The stars were out there, gleaming frostily. Far away was the constellation of Orion.

Orion ... Orion ... His thoughts began to become woolly and his limbs seemed to have enormous weights on them. There was dim confusion in his ears, which grew to a drowning roar of sound —

Then he was moving, light as thistledown. He seemed to have no body. He was hurtling through space, many times faster than the speed of light, infinitely faster than any rocket projectile could ever travel. Outwards, ever outwards, where everything was soundless and stars and suns winked with blinding intensity in the airlessness of space.

Earth was fast receding. In a matter of seconds he was beyond Pluto, on the rim of the solar system. And still he moved on, flashing with the speed of thought towards the mighty mist that was the Milky Way.

He found himself studying it in curious detachment, as though this incredible journey was a perfectly normal thing. The great infinity of stars and nebulae that made up the Milky Way Galaxy was split by holes of darkness, darker than space itself. There was the great Cleft in Argo, the Coal Sack, the Black Hole of Cygnus, and those gaping darknesses near Canis Major. For some inexplicable reason those weird abysses where no star gleamed had a fascination for him — a fascination which was only broken as he saw Orion racing out of the void to meet him.

Rigel, Betelgeuse, distant Aldebaran, brilliant blue-white Sirius: they were all there like the lanterns of God Himself, blazing sentinels amidst the lesser luminaries.

Orion . . . It was no longer a constellation. He had come too close to it for that. He could see planets, seven worlds swinging round mighty, ruddy Betelgeuse, worlds so far away from Earth that no telescope had ever glimpsed them. How could they when even their parent sun, Betelgeuse, appeared no larger than a pinpoint?

But now Betelgeuse was a magnificent sun, his colour varying constantly between deep red and brilliant orange. Here was a sun with a diameter of 300-million miles, and with a bulk 40-millon times greater than the Earth's own sun. A monarch of the void indeed.

Martin felt himself still moving, down towards the world third in order from Betelgeuse. He caught a glimpse of landscape bathed in that fantastic orange glare. There were majestic cities, pale blue oceans, clouds here and there. Mountains, plains, forests — everything a mature planet should possess . . .

It was dark.

2

Planet of the Dreamers

The darkness passed. There were sounds, just like the clicking of Elsie Barlow's heels as she had sped down the street at the close of her abrupt farewell. Martin smiled as he recalled it; then the remembrance seemed oddly blurred, like something seen in a mirror that has gradually become steamed.

'Cran! Cran, wake up! The invaders are approaching!'

Martin stirred a little and frowned to himself, still keeping his eyes closed.

'Cran, how much longer are you going to lie here and do nothing? Wake up! Wake up!'

It was the voice of a woman, apparently a young one, and a very pleasing voice it was. It had a musical lilt: but there was nothing musical about the way a hand suddenly grabbed Martin's shoulder and shook it violently.

'Hold on!' he protested, opening his eyes. 'I'm — '

He stopped dead, shut his eyes, then opened them again. He was going mad. There was no other answer. He was lying amidst silken cushions in the mightiest hall he had ever seen. It receded so far into distance he could hardly see the end of it. It was lighted by Betelgeuse casting his blazing orange-red brilliance through a curious type of glass that entirely covered the immensely lofty roof. Pillars of mighty size supported this roof and they stood, eight a side, along the magnificently carved walls.

There were endless machines walking about, apparently caring for hundreds of other men and women sprawled on silken cushions.

'I'm going off it,' Martin muttered.

'What did you say?'

This made him open his eyes again. The girl who had shaken him into life was considering him in puzzled interest. Martin took a second look at her and kept his eyes open. She was perhaps twenty-five and dressed in flowing white garments caught in at her slim waist with a glittering-jewelled belt. The crossover bands between her breasts and the rounded bare arms suggested a Grecian tendency. On her small feet were gilded sandals. Her hair, swept back from a wide and intelligent forehead, was as yellow as corn and dropped to her shoulder blades. She had beauty, even though she looked annoyed. A heart-shaped face, kissable mouth, rounded chin, and eyes of an extraordinary orange shade.

'What did you say?' she repeated.

'I — er — I'm not sure. What did you say, anyway? Something about invaders?'

'They are reported to be seven million miles distant and approaching our world rapidly.'

'Oh.' Martin wondered vaguely what he was supposed to do about it. Then he said, 'You know, you have a look of Elsie Barlow about you. I can't quite place it.'

The girl's expression of puzzled inquiry deepened. 'Cran, what is the matter with you?' she demanded. 'Do you dream so much that you have to go on doing it even when you are awake? Don't you understand? There is terrible danger threatening our whole world, and all you do is sleep — and dream — and then sleep again! What kind of a ruler are you?'

'Ruler?' Martin sat up with a jerk, and realized almost with embarrassment that he was wearing exceptionally brief trunks and a sleeveless blouse. In fact he was not sure if he was still himself. He had never noticed before what mighty arms he possessed, or that his thighs and calves were so muscular. He stood up and received another shock.

He had judged the girl was about five feet nine — his own accustomed level of height — yet now he towered over her by head and shoulders.

'Cran, what is it?' There was a plaintive note in her soft voice. Her gentle hands caught at his. 'Every time you awaken from the long sleep you seem so strange — but never so strange as now. Must I say it again? The invaders — '

'I heard you. They're seven million miles off and coming this way at the hell of a lick.'

'Hell of a lick?' the girl repeated, her eyes wide. 'You speak in a strange manner!'

'When in Rome — ' Martin began, and checked himself.

'If you hesitate much longer, Cran, we'll be destroyed,' the girl reminded him. 'Don't forget you were asleep when the last invasion came but remote control saved us. It may not be so easy this time. There are far more in this fleet than in the last one.'

'About how many?' he asked, for want of something to say.

'At least ten nirina.'

'That's a help,' Martin said, baffled, and looked into the girl's enquiring tawny eyes.

'You have only to say the word,' she said. 'Why do you hesitate?'

'Because — because I'm all clogged up!' Martin snorted. 'I can't think straight. What word do I say? If it will help I'll do it — '

'Then do it!' the girl entreated, and waited.

Silence. In the distance the queer

machines on legs with long tendrils for arms were moving soundlessly. One of them headed for Martin and he watched it warily. He was prepared to battle as the robot came close, but all the object did was reach forth a small pad of absorbent material and dab Martin gently on the brow.

'I'll be triple damned!' Martin murmured, his face blank. 'Can't a man even get a moist forehead without these ironmongery stores interfering?'

'Oh, Cran, why do you delay so?' the girl asked helplessly. 'We have so little time! Tell the machines to fight. They will only do it for you. You are the ruler: nobody else has the authority, or the vocal wave.'

Martin raised an eyebrow. The attendant robot was drifting around, ready to do his pad-dabbing act. It was curious how it made no sounds. It seemed to float more than move.

'Speak!' the girl insisted desperately.

'Eh? Oh, sorry. Just thinking — Er — fight!' Martin roared. 'To your stations! Stop the invaders!'

The things that happened after that made him watch in spellbound amazement. Through the mighty hall, from regions he could only guess at, there streamed a six-deep file of robots, all of them with legs working rhythmically, lensed eyes glinting in the diffused sunlight. They passed through a nearby opening until every one of them had gone. There must have been at least five thousand of them. They left behind the attendant robots who attended to the dozens of men and women sprawled on the silken cushions.

'I suppose those robots will be able to deal with these invaders?' Martin asked presently.

'Of course.' The girl's voice sounded colourless. 'They will use the usual eight dimensions and so destroy our foes by separating their molecular units into different time-quadrants. The eighth dimensional shield is a most efficient weapon.'

'So it sounds.'

'I wish, though, we could fight for ourselves. We are young, Cran, and if it were not for you we might behave as becomes the young. Instead you prefer this life of eternal rest, everything mechanically produced. I sometimes think your father's heritage of a perfect civilization was not a good thing. One can be — too perfect.'

Martin was silent, surveying her superb body and the beauty of her face. She was radiating some kind of seductive perfume, too. With an effort he moved away and strolled across the polished floor to where the nearest men and women were lying. They were sprawled in utter comfort, some with electrodes fastened to their heads and robots controlling the current from portable machines. Others were being fed by tubes.

'Your mechanical heritage, Cran . . . '

Martin turned as he noticed the girl had caught up with him. 'Every emotion produced synthetically. Food taken by injection; dreams induced by hypnosis; the pleasures and signs of the carnal frame created by the correct application to the nerve centres concerned. One can live and die without ever moving from the cushions. That isn't achievement, Cran: it is stagnation, demoralization, and death!'

'I think you're right,' he said absently, and at that the girl looked at him in wonder.

'But you have never agreed with me before! You have always considered me ridiculous to even mention it.'

'Maybe I haven't seen things in quite the same way before.'

The girl hesitated. 'Cran, I still cannot quite fathom your attitude. Normally you have so little time for me, even though I am your queen. You prefer to lie amongst your cushions and enjoy the pleasures of the senses, which the robots can provide. You have had none of the spirit of our ancestors — those who fought the elements and Nature to build this mighty civilization — only to hand it to absolute laziness and sloth.'

Martin had not heard half of the girl's remarks. He asked a question. 'You — you are my queen?'

'Well, of course! You cannot have forgotten the ceremony!'

'I'm afraid I have. I've been . . . out of touch.'

32

'Yes — sleeping. I know.' The girl's voice had chilled again. 'Let me repeat for your benefit that we were betrothed in this very hall six lina ago. All were awakened to witness the ceremony. At that moment I became Vola the First, Queen of Hytro, subservient only to my master, Cran Zalto. Yourself. After that you did nothing but sleep.'

'I should have my head examined,' Martin murmured.

'Why do you keep saying such strange things?' Vola demanded.

'Because, my dear, I am not the man you think. As a gentleman I must be absolutely frank with you . . . I am not your husband, and you didn't marry me. I'm a chap called Martin Clegg and I belong to Earth. How I got here God knows!'

Vola smiled compassionately. 'You are indeed over-wrought after your sleeping, Cran. There can be no doubt you are the man I married. Your magnetic aura proves it. See . . . '

She held up her dainty hand and Martin noticed she was wearing a curious but magnificent ring. It contained a huge jewel like a ruby, which was glowing with sullen fires. 'As long as you live and are Cran Zalto this jewel will glow,' she explained. 'Your body aura, wherever you may be, will excite it. If you die, or are usurped, it will become dead stone. There can be no mistake, Cran: the rulers of a race cannot afford them. No other being can ever pose as you, no matter how identical — nor can any woman ever pose as me because you, too, have your ring.'

Martin looked at his right hand and gave a start. Before he had only noticed he had one or two jewels on his finger. But now he came to look properly he saw that he also had a ruby filled with glowing fire.

'Well — er — that makes it conclusive, doesn't it?' he asked. 'Apparently I did marry you, but I cannot remember it.'

'That is hardly likely when you sleep so much.'

Martin moved slightly and put an arm about the girl's soft shoulders. He began to lead her gently back towards the bed of cushions on which he awakened. To the rear, ready for instant action, floated the robot-attendant.

'Vola, there is much that must be explained,' Martin said. 'Much that you and I do not understand.'

'Such as?'

'In spite of jewels on your fingers, in spite of this set which looks like some fantastic dream, I am *not* Cran Zalto, though it is possible that I am his twin. As I told you earlier, I belong to Earth.'

'And where is Earth?'

'Untold light years from here. Unless you have telescopes of terrific power you'd never see it. The last thing I remember is taking sleeping tablets — then I had a sort of dream, which brought me here. I awakened at your voice. The thing I want to do now is *stay* awake and find out what all this is about.'

Martin settled down on the cushions and the girl coiled her rounded body sinuously beside him. Her tawny eyes searched his face.

'Either you speak of a dream or are incredibly changed,' she pronounced at length. 'Tell me everything — in detail. I may perhaps understand.'

'I doubt if you will — but here goes.'

Martin gave her the story in detail and shrugged his huge shoulders when he had finished.

'So there it is,' he sighed. 'I find myself on another world, about which I don't know a single thing. I also find myself talking your language with perfect ease and learn that I am married to you, that I am the ruler of a super-perfect race. It's both baffling and — as far as you are concerned — embarrassing.'

Vola gave her gentle, understanding smile. 'Whether you are Cran or not,' she said, 'you have all the instincts of a gentleman, and for that I respect you. But the fact remains that you are Cran because you never moved from your cushions during your sleep. However, scientific matters as deep as this are beyond me.'

She turned and looked at the robot. 'Fetch XK,' she ordered, and the robot moved away dutifully.

'Who is XK?' Martin asked warily.

'A robot with fifteen of the best brains

linked by reason of their frequency sympathy. Neither of you lived properly. Your twin on Earth was partly you, and you were partly him. In his case it took the form of discontent and bad dreams; in your case it made you apathetic and unresponsive to the vital situations of the moment. You sought solace in the induced emotions of our endless machines and neglected everything else, including your queen. Now your twin has ceased to be a factor you are the real Cran, with your mind balanced and your emotions no longer disturbed.'

'So that's it,' Martin said, musing. 'I have really been Cran all the time? The Earth business was just a dream?'

'A vivid one — so vivid you seemed to live as the Earth man lived.'

'Then how is it I cannot remember anything of what I should know? About this planet, I mean — and Vola. For all I understand of the situation I might just as well have only just got here.'

'The brain twinship would create a form of amnesia. That is understandable when you reflect that you lived two lives simultaneously.'

'I understand this language. How is that?'

'Because it is your language. So you instinctively know it.'

'Whilst I was Martin Clegg,' Martin continued, looking bothered, 'I kept sensing a tremendous urgency. As though somebody were calling me to come here. Can you explain that?'

'Yes. It was the voice and mind of Vola trying to awaken you from sleep to combat the invasion that still threatens. She succeeded — or at least you awoke, if only because your twin decided to surrender his consciousness.'

There was silence. The girl made a movement with her hand and in response XK turned about and silently left the great hall. The gentle tentacles of the robot smoothed the cushions out behind the girl as she stretched in languorous comfort.

'So simple when explained,' she said, smiling.

'Yes . . . I only hope that bag of wires is right. I have the feeling that everything is

40

most . . . well, unethical. In regard to you and me, I mean. Our marriage, for instance.'

'You cannot mean, now you have recovered your full personality, that you dislike me, Cran?' Something like tears began to appear in Vola's tawny eyes.

'Lord, no! No man in his right senses could do that. I — I just feel a heel, that's all.'

'Heel? Would it make you any happier if the ceremony were performed over again?'

Martin grinned. 'That's the only suggestion which has made sense to me so far. By all means! Sooner the better.'

'Arrange a ceremony,' the girl told the robot, and it drifted away silently. Then another robot came speeding inwards and halted at the cushions.

'Invasion repelled, Excellence,' it announced. 'The oncoming armada has been disrupted into the time-quadrants.'

'Good show,' Martin approved, far more interested in Vola than a mysterious armada which had been disintegrated. Vola motioned a hand and then looked at

Martin seriously.

'There will be other invasions, Cran,' she said, her expression troubled. 'One day we may be attacked by scientists who will be too clever for us. That is the thing I fear. Our civilization is standing still because it has achieved perfection. It just cannot get any higher. If there is a real menace which may wipe us out, only you can prevent it.'

'How?'

'That is for you to decide, as ruler.'

Martin stirred himself a little. Delectable though Vola certainly was there were other issues with which he had to get to grips.

'Am I to understand,' he asked slowly, 'that on this world there is only one civilization, so utterly perfect that everything can afford to lie down and let robots do everything for them? Is every conceivable emotion stimulated mechanically?'

'Yes. Those who prefer it otherwise and who like to fight for themselves as the pioneers of this civilization did are considered as Retrogrades. I am one of them, even though I am your queen.'

'By which you mean you don't like artificial stimulation? You prefer — to put it bluntly — to be up and doing?'

'All the time. I like to live like a healthy young woman. I like to sleep like one. I like to achieve, to do things, to master problems — to be myself. It was the bitterest disappointment to me when I found you were one of the Sleepers.'

'But I'm not now,' Martin pointed out. 'I quite agree with you that we should stand on our own two feet. When you have things done for you all the time it leads to decadence and death — just as you said a while back. You can rest assured, Vola. I have too much of Martin Clegg, Earthman, in me to allow me to go to sleep on the job. Though how one improves an already perfect civilization is hard to visualize.'

'The point is,' Vola answered deliberately, 'that other civilizations on neighbouring worlds know we are a sleepy race — and therefore we become the target for their depredations. So far we have smashed every attack. More will come. But greatest of all looms a problem we must solve. How to save our world from the Black Terror.'

Martin raised an eyebrow enquiringly.

'You have already seen it, surely? It lies in the nebulae, amongst the stars. It is eating away the Universe — '

The girl could not proceed any further for at that moment several robots of intermediate size entered. Under their gentle guidance the men and women on the cushions were aroused from slumber and supported with tentacle arms as they were formed into groups. When this was over a man of magnificent stature and attired in superb robes came into view.

'Our dispenser of law and judgment,' Vola murmured, as she and Martin stood up side by side. 'He will re-perform the marriage rites and our retinue here will be witnesses.'

'How many living people are there on this world?' Martin murmured.

'Exactly one million — the finest of the race. The rest were destroyed.'

Upon this ruthless though probably logical policy Martin had nothing to say. He watched the Dispenser come to within a few feet and he bowed majestically.

Throughout the length of the vast hall the men and women stood waiting, and watching, some of them yawning with the effort of keeping awake.

The ceremony was brief and included many words that Martin did not understand. At the end of if he embraced Vola tightly and the Dispenser departed with dignified tread. By the time Martin had at last released the girl he found that all the men and women had relaxed again on their cushions. Cooling fans were being wafted above them by the robots.

'Of all the lazy, spineless, shiftless lot I ever struck this crowd in here takes the bun,' Martin murmured; then he gave the girl a sharp glance. 'How comes it that you don't behave like the rest of them?'

'I am descended from pioneers,' she answered proudly. 'I would rather die in defeated action than live in a dream state where nothing real ever happens.'

'I suppose we have a big city here?' Martin asked.

'The biggest. This city is the capital of Hytro. Hytro is the name of our world, of course.'

'Any way in which I can view it without these confounded robots carrying me around piecemeal?'

'Certainly. Come with me.'

Vola turned and led the way from the enormous room, informing the robots as she went that attendance would not be required. It was leaving the room and following the endless corridors, which gave Martin a good idea of the size of the building. It must have covered several square miles. Finally the girl entered an elevator, which, by automatic means, rose to the roof. Martin found himself emerging into the glare of mighty Betelgeuse.

He shaded his eyes and looked about him, then followed the girl's graceful form across the roof to the parapet. Here he stood and silently surveyed. As he had guessed earlier, the city was enormous, composed not of dozens of separate edifices but one or two colossal ones, in which — presumably — many other buildings were incorporated.

In general the view was not unlike one on Earth, except for the design of the buildings. They had a beauty surpassing anything any Earth architect had ever dreamed of. But everything else appeared normal — the broad, park-like spaces, the street filled with robots or mechanical vehicles, the distant range of mountains, the pale blue ocean perhaps three miles away. And overhead the cobalt sky, with Betelgeuse pouring down his torrid heat and orange-red light . . .

'A pleasant enough world,' Martin commented at length, his survey complete. 'And thank heaven it has an oxygen-nitrogen atmosphere otherwise I'd be dead by now.'

'All the planets have oxy-nitrogen atmospheres,' the girl answered. 'You can't see them now in the daylight, but at night they are plainly visible. Only a matter of three million miles separates us from the nearest one.'

'And was it from there that the invasion came?'

Vola shook her blonde head. 'No. All the six planets around this one are dead. Their peoples achieved perfection long before us and died because of that perfection. That is why I do not want it to happen to our world, the last in the group. No,' she continued, 'the invasion came from out of the greater depths. From the Galaxy itself.'

'Meaning the Milky Way?'

'If that is a term your other self might use — yes. I refer to that enormous field of misty light, that titanic ocean of star dust and worlds unborn, so near to this world of ours.'

'And what made them pick on this planet?'

'Because it is next in line to theirs. They will always come this way, seeking a place where they can temporarily rest before the Black Terror drives them on again.'

Martin rubbed the back of his head. 'This Black Terror business puzzles me, Vola. What's it exactly?'

'The death of the Universe, unless there arises a mind powerful enough to defeat it. Come — I will show you.'

The girl led the way back across the room to the elevator. It went down one flight and there stopped. In a moment, or two Martin found himself walking into the biggest observatory he had ever seen, its only ceiling the sky. Here there was telescopic equipment of every conceivable type, and most of it advanced in design beyond his wildest imagination.

Vola gave an order to the scientist in charge — a grave, impersonal being of indeterminable age, dressed in the prevailing fashion of short trunks and sleeveless blouse.

'We would view the First Galaxy,' Vola said briefly. 'And the Black Terror — Focus it on the screens.'

'Yes, Highness,' the astronomer assented, and settled himself at a control board.

Motors droned and instruments swung around in universal mountings. On a tiny screen the astronomer obtained a pilot-image on the object he was seeking. He switched it through to a giant screen on the wall and then pressed a button. Immediately light-polarizing beams flashed horizontally from side to side of the roof, turning the observatory into total darkness.

'There you see the Black Terror,' Vola announced, and put her hand on a control knob with which she could change the view on the screen any moment she wished.

Martin found himself looking at an enormously magnified picture of the Milky Way. He recognized it easily enough and marvelled at the telescopic equipment which made the view so clear even in broad daylight. There was no gainsaying that huge band of light flooded with countless millions of stars . . . Then as the view changed there came onto the screen a deep black area, even darker than space itself, just as he had seen it in his mysterious mental plunge through the void.

'That,' Vola said, her voice taut, 'is an example of the Black Terror. An area where nothing is. Total absence of all matter, all light, all anything. Through the centuries it has spread, and now its speed has suddenly increased. Far away in the outer dark it is destroying everything before it. Matter itself is dying.'

'That space there is what we call — on Earth I mean — the 'Coal Sack',' Martin said, thinking. 'There are other blank

50

areas too — the Black Hole of Cygnus, the Great Cleft of Argo, regions where nothing exists . . . And you believe something is destroying matter?'

'We know it is, but everybody has been too sleepy to work out why. I have tried, and failed. The fifteen-brain robot has wrestled with the problem and arrived at no conclusion. Now only you can perhaps solve it.'

Martin gave an incredulous smile. 'I'm afraid your faith in me won't run to that, Vola!'

'Look at that Galaxy,' she continued, the view sweeping over it as she moved the controls. 'It is full of huge caverns of emptiness, pits of darkness in which life has died. Those worlds directly in line with this unknown something have also been destroyed. That is why armadas keep flying this way — fleeing from this Black Terror. Our world is one worth living upon for a brief while, so these invaders think, until the Terror has reached this far. That is why there will be more fugitives seeking to destroy and conquer, if only to gain a brief respite from disaster . . . '

She switched off suddenly. The daylight returned. There was an unexpected intensity in her expression.

'When, in your dream self, you experienced that sense of urgency, Cran, it was me urging you to save us,' she continued. 'I have known for a long time it can only be a matter of years before this Black Terror catches up with us. Then it will sweep on like an infinite tide, destroying everything in its path. For some inexplicable reason the Universe is dying. Matter is being utterly destroyed.'

'And you expect me to find the answer to that?' Martin asked blankly.

'I believe you can, if you will apply yourself. You have the heritage of a long line of geniuses — the geniuses who built this miraculous civilization in which we live. Do you wish to see it all destroyed?'

Martin took the girl's arm gently. 'Look, Vola, I'm a perfectly ordinary fellow with very little scientific knowledge. I may have sprung from geniuses, but it certainly missed a beat in my generation —'

'It didn't, Cran, it didn't!' Vola's tawny

eyes were bright with contradiction. 'You still haven't shaken off that other personality — that most ordinary of creatures to whom you were linked on Earth. Here is a problem as majestic as the Universe itself and it is given to you to solve it. You can because you must. You have said you will fight, as I wish to do: now is your chance to do it. I'll always be with you, battling at your side. If our world is destroyed it is the end of everything that has been built up . . . '

3

Mental Colossus

Suddenly all sense of flippancy left Martin. He realized with startling clearness that he was not just some transferred being from Earth who, accidentally, had been given a lovely woman for a wife. He was not a man who could spend his days lounging in silken cushions and doing just whatever he liked. He was a ruler, and ahead of him and all those who owed him allegiance was a something that blotted out worlds and stars with a terrible completeness.

'I would like to study space through this telescopic equipment,' he said at length. 'Preferably by night.'

'Day or night, Cran, it makes no difference.'

'It does to me. I might wish to compare the sky as it looks to my naked eye. If I am to make a beginning on this problem

I must see what it comprises.'

'Tonight then,' Vola agreed. 'That will give you time to refresh and change. In the stress of things I had forgotten such simple matters. The robots will do all you wish.'

They did, almost to Martin's embarrassment. They bathed and dressed him and brushed his hair. To his surprise he found no shaving was necessary: his beard and moustache had become extinct, which made him feel infernally emasculated.

After the palaver he was carried to his silken cushions in the arms of a robot and laid down. Soft tubes were attached to veins in his arm. Then he noticed Vola in a similar mountain of cushions nearby.

'You like this sort of thing?' he asked her.

'I loathe it. But if one has perfection I suppose there is no other course.'

'No?' Martin's eyes glinted. Suddenly he jumped to his feet, picked up the nearest cushion, and hurled it at the robot who was just about to feed him.

'Get to hell out of here!' Martin roared.

'When I want to eat I'll feed myself!'

The effect of his violent thought waves upon the delicate receiving mechanisms of the robots was catastrophic. They reeled about like toys hanging on strings caught suddenly in a draught. They lost all sense of balance and went spinning giddily into corners or crashed on the floor out of commission.

Martin stood glaring at them, his feet apart, his huge fists clenched.

'You have broken the mental contact, Cran,' Vola said, rising slowly and looking about her. 'The robots were geared to obey only the sleepy, low-pitched frequency of the dreamers, of which you were one, and — '

'There aren't going to be any dreamers any more!' Cran retorted. 'That's over, finished with — just the way you wanted it. You're young, and so am I, and we've too much to do to spend our time being spoon-fed. And that goes for the rest of this lazy mob, too.'

He strode forward against the reclining men and women. Without any ceremony he seized them by arms or shoulders dragged them on their feet. By the time he had finished some hundred or so were swaying upright and looking about them, in bewilderment. Martin eyed them and then strode to a position where he could address them.

'Now, my friends, listen to me,' he said deliberately. 'I am the ruler of this world and I have decided on the way it shall be run. I know I have indulged the pleasures of the dream world as much as you have, and therefore I am not blaming you for having — until now — led the life of lotus-eaters. But now it is finished. Too much perfection can be dangerous. When everything is done for you initiative dies. We are going to recover the spirit of the men and women who built this civilization. We are going to fight our own battles — particularly when invaders dare to come near our planet. What is more we are going to discover how to save our world from a tide of ruin which is sweeping in from the depths of the Universe.'

The men and women, all of them young and magnificent specimens, looked at each other. Then one of them spoke:

'But, Excellency, it was upon your orders that we became Dreamers. You said we must do as you did and enjoy the fruits of perfection.'

'I am entitled to change my mind, and have done so. Henceforth you will do whatever is required of you and dreaming shall cease. I will determine shortly what task each one of you shall fulfill. Until then you will spend your time travelling to all parts of this planet arousing others who may be in a similar condition of torpor. That understood?'

The men and women nodded humbly.

'Then go,' Martin ordered. 'By the time you have returned I shall have delegated you to special tasks.'

He watched the men and women file out of the huge chamber, then with a grim smile he returned to where Vola was standing, her eyes bright.

'That was wonderful, Cran!' she declared, gripping his arm. 'I knew you could do it if you would only arouse yourself. Come, let us eat in the normal way for the first time in your period of rule.'

Still holding on to his arm she led him from the great room into an adjoining one. At her orders a robot brought normal food and laid it on the table, together with wines and essences. By the time the meal was over the glare of Betelgeuse was dying away and soft lighting had taken its place.

'How long does this planet take to revolve?' Martin asked.

'Twenty-five kinfas,' Vola answered, and after some questioning Martin managed to discover a kinfa was about the equivalent of an Earth-hour.

'That gives me plenty of time to study,' he said. 'Since I do not feel the need of sleep — and I shouldn't after the amount of it I've had since becoming ruler! — I'm going to spend the night studying space . . . I suppose there is no better way to do it than from the observatory? It only enables me to see one part of the heavens at a time.'

'We can take an observation machine into the void if you wish.'

Martin nodded decisively, getting to his feet and following Vola through the maze of corridors until they reached what was obviously a private hangar. Within it were a dozen gleaming projectile-like machines. It required no imagination on Martin's part to guess that they were spaceships of extremely advanced design.

'For a ruler, and one supposed to know everything, I ask an awful lot of questions,' he apologized. 'Do these travel by atomic force or rocket recoil?'

'Neither. They utilize magnetic lines of force, which exist in an inconceivably fine mesh throughout the Universe. The basis of these machines is repulsion. In their endeavours to fly away from the magnetic lines of force — on the law of like repulsing like — they achieve stupendous velocity. They can, if necessary, move at three hundred thousand miles a second — in your terms of measurement and time — when surrounded by other matter, such as planets, when caution is necessary. But, with absolutely free inter-galactic space in which to move a velocity of a million miles a second is not impossible.'

Martin swallowed hard. 'But — but

that's infinitely faster than light itself!'

Vola nodded. 'Much faster. Light is not the ultimate speed of the Universe by any means. The fastest known velocity is that achieved by thought. You had an experience of that in your own mental crossing of space from your world to here . . . One of these machines can traverse the Universe if need be, and not take very long about it either. However, we are wasting time and you have observations you wish to make.'

Vola entered the roomy control room and closed the airlock after Martin had followed her in. The movement of a button sent forth a vibration that swung back the hangar roof. The stars and Milky Way had replaced it — the unfamiliar sky as seen from this world so near to Betelgeuse.

Then under the movement of a switch the machine leapt into the void and 'leapt' was the only word for it. In a matter of seconds it seemed to be hundreds of miles away in space, simply falling upwards instead of downwards and leaving behind it a night-swathed planet.

Martin moved to the window and looked out onto the heavens towards which the vessel was hurtling, then he looked away quickly as from behind the world they had left Betelgeuse suddenly appeared — blinding, enormous, devouring, the inconceivable blaze of his corona stretching untold millions of miles into space.

Looking the other way Martin was faced with the First Galaxy, the Milky Way, with its caverns of darkness. Then there were stars that he could roughly place. He recognized Vega, Lyra, Cepheus, Castor, Pollux, Procyon . . . Endless hosts of them.

Then Vola had set the automatic control and come to his side. She moved easily, the terrific acceleration miraculously counteracted by inertia-nullifiers in the floor, leaving only a normal gravity effect.

'If you wish to observe the Black Terror you have no better place than here,' she said. 'See through this . . . '

She set a telescopic device in action, which, upon a circle of polished, reflective substance, cast a pin-sharp image of the void ahead. Martin studied it intently. He could see stars and nebulae distinctly — for a certain distance; then as the light centuries increased in range there was nothing but the Dark, the everlasting Dark, in which nothing gleamed. Just one awful abyss towards which the little machine was hurtling with inconceivable velocity.

'We are looking into remoteness, Cran,' Vola said, speaking of the Dark beyond the stars. 'Out there is the absolute rim of the Universe. At one time it was thick with stars and planets — but they have all gone. Every one, like lights foundering in an ocean. Our own graphs and plates show this Dark to be hurtling inwards at fantastic speed.'

'And as it advances the inhabitants of other worlds get out quickly and come this way — away from it?' Martin questioned.

'Those who can — yes. Those who have no means of interstellar space travel presumably are devoured by the Dark. Our world being the first inhabited one in order of progression we are subjected to endless invasions as planet after planet is threatened by this unknown something. Before very long our world too will go. Now you know the reason for urgency.'

'We have space travel,' Martin pointed out. 'What is to prevent us making an exodus, too?'

'The fact that running away from the Dark is not to defeat it. It will catch up with us in the end. Our only course is to try and make a stand against it.'

Martin said nothing. The girl's intense, tawny eyes were fixed on him. He moved slightly and shrugged.

'What am I to do, Vola? I am not a scientific genius. If the fifteen-brained robot, containing the best brains of the race, cannot master the problem, what chance do *I* stand?'

'There is a way,' Vola answered. 'It depends if you have the courage to take it.'

'Meaning?'

'Our sun, like any sun, emits radiations which are masked by the atmosphere of our planet. Some of those radiations, operating through what is called the seventh-octave, can change an ordinary being into a genius, and a genius into a mental colossus.'

'I'm afraid,' he said, 'you'll have to explain that to me more fully . . . In the meantime I suppose nothing could be gained by venturing into this Dark ahead and finding out what's in it?'

'That would mean dissolution, Cran; I'm convinced of it. Our only course is to find out its nature and then work out means of counteracting it. We had better return home and I will show you what I mean by the seventh-octave.'

Vola returned to the switchboard, took the automatic control out of commission, and then swung the fast moving vessel round in a vast arc. As it streaked back towards the planet Martin studied the Milky Way again, surveying those enormous holes that had been created inside it.

Once the city had been regained Vola led the way to the main laboratory. The living men and women and robots already at work in the huge area paid no attention to her, going on with their various tasks.

She halted finally before an instrument that reminded Martin of a full-sized cine-projector. In fact, in essence, it evidently was, for upon the snapping of a switch it projected onto a wall-screen a varicoloured band of light.

'That is the first-octave of our sun,' Vola explained. 'Infra red — the one responsible for heat. Now here are the others — two contains light-photons; three contains the orange wavebands; four the, ultra-violet; five, the colours which no eye normally sees — '

Martin blinked, as indescribable waves fluttered over the screen and made him feel dizzy.

'Six contains cosmic radiation, and this is seven . . . '

The seventh-octave, reproduced in light form, looked like a zigzag rainbow containing all the hues of the spectrum.

'Every star or sun emits this seventh-octave,' Vola explained. 'It is responsible for evolution. Because of it seeping through in very low percentage through the atmospheric deflection, the amoeba grows into a thinking being as ages pass.

Here you see it in its true form, unmasked by atmosphere, because the magnetic beam which is attracting it to this instrument projects far beyond our atmospheric range. If a living, thinking being — such as you or I — comes under the influence of this unmasked seventh-octave radiation for any length of time it causes a metamorphosis that is akin to super-evolution. In the space of hours — as you would call them — you cover centuries. You understand?'

'Only too well,' Martin assented. 'As one evolves one naturally becomes cleverer because of the development of the brain along with the body.'

'So,' Vola said quietly, switching off, 'that is the answer.'

'Are you sure it is?' Martin asked, pondering. 'Isn't all knowledge gained by inference? I mean, does it really mean that one will become cleverer just because of evolution? Isn't it necessary to learn *as* one evolves in order to improve one's knowledge?'

'No. *Real* knowledge is gained by one's brain being in sympathy with the thought sea around us. The more refined and evolved the brain the higher the knowledge.'

Martin nodded, thinking of a half forgotten memory. Tom Cavendish had outlined that very theory about the 'thought-sea'. Tom Cavendish? Did he really exist? Was there such a place as Earth? Did there live on it a girl called Elsie Barlow?

'Well?' Vola asked, waiting, and Martin gave a start.

'Sorry, Vola; just thinking of something . . . I gather you think I ought to absorb some of this seventh-octave radiation and become a genius?'

'Is there anything unpleasant about it? Knowledge is the one thing which all living beings crave.'

'Depends on the person. I'm quite happy as I am, with you, and — '

'That is the old, lazy Cran Zalto talking,' the girl interrupted sharply. 'You are a ruler, Cran, and for that reason you must sink your own desires.'

Martin looked at the instrument. 'I don't understand,' he said, 'why nobody has attempted to become a genius before now and defeat this Black Terror.'

'For the simple reason that nobody has been permitted. Only the ruler can give sanction, and that person is you. In any case the threat of the Black Terror has not been so serious as it is now . . . It is for you to make this effort to evolve Cran.'

'And what of you?'

'I will do likewise if you command it, but it would not be right for me to perhaps achieve greater mental dominance than you. I am not the ruler.'

Martin began to pace up and down restlessly, still thinking the business over carefully. The girl watched him. She was still watching him as he came to a stop.

'Is there danger in this experiment? Not that I'm afraid of that, but if anything is liable to happen to me I must delegate my powers to you.'

'That will happen automatically if anything overwhelms you. But nothing will, Cran. There is no danger in evolution. All you do is get ahead of the centuries and a living frame is made to stand that, just as the brain is made to expand. You know that a brain only uses a fifth of its real power. Evolution will make use of the remaining material: that is why it is put there.'

'Spare tyre, eh?' Martin asked dryly, and the girl looked puzzled. Then he added. 'All right, I'll try it. What do I do? Stand in the beam of this projector?'

'No: this is only the instrument for detecting the radiation. Come with me.' Vola walked across the laboratory to a gigantic machine, which, to Martin anyway, was too complicated for understanding. The only part of it that made sense to him was a giant horseshoe magnet supported on massive stanchions over a metal plate. The girl motioned to the plate and he stood on it and waited for the next.

'This machine absorbs the radiation direct from our sun,' Vola explained. 'It is passed through the transformers and escapes by the magnet. You will come directly under its influence. If for any reason you find the sensation unendurable, you have only to press this switch here,' — she indicated it — 'and the apparatus will stop dead. I know no more than that. I did not devise these wonderful machines: they are the product of the pioneers of our race and I only understand how to operate them . . . Now, are you ready?'

'Go ahead,' Martin assented. 'Can't be much worse than a visit to the dentist, I suppose.'

Plainly the girl did not understand his very Earthly comment. She shrugged and closed a switch amidst a flare of blue sparks. Martin waited, and for a moment or two felt entirely unchanged; then a sensation of overbalance seized him and he staggered helplessly. It passed almost immediately, and after that he was incapable of realizing what really did happen. It was as if something opened in his mind and a stream of ideas, thoughts, and conceptions poured into it. At the same time, though he was not aware of it himself, his body changed, too. He became less gigantic and his shoulders narrowed. But, in proportion, his head increased its size. He never once felt the need of pressing the emergency switch.

71

So, at length, the surge of mysterious power ceased and he looked about him. He felt re-born, utterly different, all the emotions he had formerly possessed having somehow deserted him. He no longer felt the urge to quip, or treat the environment of this far-flung planet with levity. Even Vola, at whom he looked steadily, only seemed to be a female and no longer a completely desirable creature. He saw her not as a woman but as a unit, fitting into the pattern of the Universe.

'Well?' she asked, gazing at him in awe.

'Apparently the experiment was successful, Vola.' Martin found himself wondering at the clipped, precise tone of his voice. 'You are to be congratulated.'

She made no response. Her eyes remained fixed on him as he stepped from the metallic stand. He considered himself for a moment and then turned.

'Apparently, by a process of metamorphosis, my body has evolved with my brain,' he said. 'Which is only what can be expected. I am slightly less in height, but my cranium is far larger.'

'Do you *feel* any more intelligent?' Vola asked anxiously.

'I feel able to grapple with fundamental problems,' he replied. 'I regret only one thing — the loss of emotions which make up a human being. Love, compassion, laughter, sadness. Those are the mixtures that make up life, Vola. They have been blasted out of me. I have traded all to become a man of supreme intelligence. I am left wondering: is it worth it?'

'There is no way back, Cran,' Vola said quietly. 'You cannot de-evolve. That is contrary to Nature.'

Martin did not answer. His massive forehead was wrinkled and as he raised a hand to it he also realized that his hair had gone. He was baldpated. It dawned on him then that with evolution hair, the most lowly attribute of a living being, would of course disappear. It was a relic of the anthropoid, anyway.

'I evolved for only one reason,' he said at length. 'To determine the nature of the Black Terror. I must begin that investigation immediately. Summon the scientists. I shall require photographs, computations, references . . . '

Vola accepted the command humbly. She had her part to play. She knew that in turning Cran Zalto into a genius she had lost a young virile husband and wedded herself to an arid, coldly scientific being in whom all emotion was dead. Such was her part of the sacrifice, and she accepted it as a woman will — with resigned calm.

For several minutes afterwards Martin paced about and rubbed his eyes and head. Confusion was still surging in his brain, even though it was settling down. He found himself thinking of all the problems he had ever known, on Earth and on this strange planet — and the startling thing was that there were no problems any more. Mathematics, geometry, dimensions — all the 'difficult' sciences he thoroughly understood. It was pleasurable to realize it, but he still did not know if he enjoyed it. He missed human emotion and the power to laugh . . .

Then the scientists he had summoned began to gather. Some of them were those who had been spending their time sleeping. Others he had never seen before. They gathered in the laboratory, Vola in their rear, and looked in silent amazement at their utterly changed ruler.

'Before us, unless we smash it, is the Black Terror,' Martin said, his voice arid and inflexible. 'I have decided that we, as a scientific and perfect race, shall not go down before it but will bend it to our will. For that reason I have evolved myself centuries ahead of the present in order that my brain may be able to grapple with the problem. Each one of you will obey my instructions, and we shall commence work immediately.'

He turned, and without having to decide which instrument was which, he delegated each of the scientists to an especial task — some to photography, others to records, still other to stellar charts, until finally he had every man and woman at a task which would help his activity. For himself he took over the mathematical machines and fed into them the pooled information he received from the workers.

Vola helped him, quietly, unobtrusively,

working as a very lowly wife before a very dominant husband. Not that he wanted it that way: he was simply ruled by the evolution that had changed him.

With scant regard for sleep or meals he kept at his task for several days and nights, showing his assistants no respite and merely smiling at their obvious weariness as time passed. So, gradually, out of the mass of information he gathered, and his own study of the void, he began to gain an exact idea of the nature of the Dark — and his discoveries left him grim.

Finally he reached the stage where he could announce his findings.

'There is only one explanation for the Black Terror,' he said. 'The Universe, as we know it, began from the explosion of a gigantic primal atom, its matter rushing outwards from the central core to form the Expanding Universe. We, of the Universe, and all other matter in it, are parts of that initial explosion. But outside of the Universe — and inside it — the central core from which the primal atom exploded, there is *nothing*. Only non-space-time.'

The scientists glanced at one another. Vola kept her eyes fixed on Martin, absorbing every word he uttered and knowing he was absolutely correct. He was too intelligent now to be capable of a mistake.

'The Universe is expanding,' Martin continued. 'That fact is admitted by all scientists wherever they may be, and no matter on what world. But mathematics postulate that there must come a time when the inner explosion will overtake the outward explosion. That means that the inner core of non-space-time will overtake the exploded matter at colossal speed. Faster than light itself, therefore faster than matter itself can move! Matter is being engulfed by non-space-time and this non-space-time expansion, moving with resistless, awful speed will eat all through matter until it joins the equal state of non-space-time existing outside the Universe . . . '

'Nothing,' he finished, 'can stop it. Now we know why the scientists of other worlds fled from before it. They could no more defeat the laws of celestial mechanics than I can. Soon the other inhabitants of other worlds will flee from the devouring Dark. They will use this world as a temporary resting place maybe — if we allow it — and then hurry on again. Always fleeing, onwards — away from the Dark. We see it now spreading its ugly emptiness on the First Galaxy. Eventually the whole Universe will be swallowed up, forced back into the state of non-space-time which existed before matter was.'

In the still unbroken silence Vola's voice asked a question.

'Cran, did you say that nothing can stop it?' she asked.

He looked at her bleakly. 'Yes, that is what I said.'

'You, who have gained more intelligence than any of us, admit you are defeated?'

'One cannot stop the movement of elemental forces,' he replied brusquely. 'Do you think I have not measured this problem, have not pondered it from every aspect? Celestial mechanics forbid our interference. Don't you understand, it is the death of the Universe? Just as it was born, so it must die. The inevitable cycle.

To an explosion, be it great or small, there must come quiescence when the explosion has spent itself . . . We can do nothing.'

Vola was silent, sheer dismay on her beautiful face. Then Martin clenched his fist, a faraway look in his eyes.

'I am wondering.' he mused, 'how it all began? Whence came the primal atom, which now threatens us with destruction because its power is less swift than the non-space-time that bore it? How do Universes begin? There is a problem worthy of my genius.'

'But not as essential as our survival,' Vola pointed out.

4

Into the Darkness

Martin seemed about to comment when the sound of the alarm siren aroused him. Immediately the scientists began moving urgently, studying the instruments that gave them a view of space and all parts of their planet.

'Invasion imminent!' came a mechanical voice through the loudspeaker. 'Invasion armada approaching from eastern sector of space. Vessels number eighteen jendors.'

'Which is thirty thousand machines,' Martin interpreted. 'They can do plenty of damage in those numbers — if we let them. But I imagine they are going to have a surprise.'

'You have some method devised for defeating them?' Vola asked, her voice dispirited as she still remembered Martin's statement that he could not defeat the Black Terror.

'I am determined to teach these invaders a lesson,' he retorted. 'It may serve as a warning to the inhabitants of other planets if they think of stopping here — for I have no doubt we are watched telescopically all the time . . . To your stations,' he ordered the scientists. 'You have already been instructed in what you must do.'

The scientists began moving to various types of machines and settled themselves in the seats before them. Hands poised over banks of control keys waiting for Martin's orders. He for his part studied the screens that gave him view of outer space. In the midst of it, clearly lighted by Betelgeuse, was the approaching armada, vast and majestic, and travelling at high speed.

'What have you devised?' Vola asked, gripping Martin's arm. 'Is it an improvement on the robot defenses we formerly had?'

'I imagine so.' He turned to look at her. 'I have created a *mathematical* defense. The basic energy quanta of those ships will be rendered void because the mathematical postulations making up their atoms will be cancelled out. My defense is based on the probability wave of the electron, incorporating seven dimensions.'

This was a range of science over which Vola stumbled, for all her knowledge. It made her realize, even with a slight feeling of fear, how completely Martin had evolved from the bewildered young man who had awakened on the cushions. Silent, she remained at his side, watching the invaders sweep ever nearer.

'Prepare . . . ' Martin ordered, raising his hand.

Switches closed. The hum of powerful generators pervaded the laboratory. Martin listened to the sound climbing to maximum, then he dropped his hand in the signal.

Instantly there flashed out from Hytro an invisible wall of mathematical vibrations, and because it *was* invisible the invaders had no chance to prepare. The effect, seen on the viewing screens, was startling. There was no suggestion of an explosion, no flashing of light or a crumbling of machines. It seemed as though the entire fleet floated into transparency and then no longer existed.

'What happened?' Vola asked blankly, staring. 'I never saw so complete a disappearance.'

'The perfect weapon,' Martin said, with a hard smile, giving the signal to cut off the power. 'Everything in the Universe is mathematical at root. Work out the correct equations, and their attendant vibrations, and you can cancel out any set of mathematics you desire. That is what I did — so, of course, the armada ceased to exist when cancellation overwhelmed it.'

'You, who can think of such a plan to protect our world, yet find the Black Terror beyond you?' Vola shook her golden haired head slowly. 'I find it hard to understand, Cran.'

'Perhaps,' he mused, 'I am not clever enough . . . yet.'

Vola looked at him sharply. There was that faraway look in his eyes again. His fists were clenched as he stood brooding.

'You have evolved to the limit — ' she began, but he cut her short.

'No, Vola. I have only evolved a quarter of the distance I might yet go. I am wondering what lies at the end of the road, when one has evolved so far that there is nothing left. Would one not become a mental ultimate?'

Vola said nothing. She could read the devouring ambition in his expression. The flawless way in which he had defeated a threatened invasion had done something to him, magnified his already great conception of his own importance.

'Even if you evolved to the limit, there is no guarantee you would even then defeat the Black Terror,' Vola said at last. 'And in evolving you would lose the last shreds of human structure and become solely a coldly logical, utterly scientific brain. I beg of you not to go that far.'

'Why not?' he demanded. 'Since I have been deprived of all other emotions what else is left for me but evolution, and the achievements which spring from it?'

'*What* achievements?' the girl asked helplessly. 'What is there left when our world, when all the Universe is doomed to destruction in all too short a time?'

'Did it never occur to you,' Martin asked slowly, 'that one might create a world?'

The question was such a colossal one Vola had no answer for it. Martin took her arm — not with the gentleness he had once expressed but with a firm, compelling grip. There was no longer any kindly emotion left in him. He knew exactly what he wanted and expected implicit obedience. He held on to Vola until they had reached the sun-saturated terrace that lay beyond the laboratory.

'That's better,' he said, releasing her. 'One can breathe more freely here, and those other clods do not need to listen to what I have to say. I tell it to you, Vola, because you are my wife, not because I think you will understand.'

Vola almost made a hot retort at the slight upon her intelligence, and then hesitated. It would be lost on Martin completely.

'I believe,' he said, 'that one should never admit defeat: one should make use of it. But in this case it will demand the absolute essence of intelligence to bring my plan to success . . . Since we are faced with annihilation, we must create another Universe, and other worlds, and select from those worlds one which will appeal to us. Upon it, scientifically, we can create a race. We — '

'Cran . . . ' Vola put a hand on his arm gently. 'Cran, you are getting way beyond all reason. To have genius is one thing: to dream of the impossible is another.'

'It is not impossible!' he snapped, glaring at her. 'In the dim Beginning of time somebody created a Universe. They must have done. Otherwise, how did it get there?'

'Somebody?' Vola shook her head. 'Some *thing*, Cran. You are getting beyond all reason with your theories. Science admits that it can only explain how things work, not how they are created.'

'Science, Vola, exists because it is the only law of the Universe. Let me tell you something — a quotation I remember from when I was on Earth. It was uttered by a very great scientist called Jeans. He said, as near as I can recall it, that in the

Beginning there was non-space-time, a condition where nothing is, where nothing ever happens, where there is total Absence. Some super-scientist *outside* this state of non-space-time *willed* a Universe into being. In a void of non-space-time the impact of thought waves would crystallize because it would be a random element in an otherwise undisturbed state. That crystallization would produce coarse matter, and a primal atom would be formed. Can you understand that?'

'Yes, I can understand it.'

'Very well then. What one scientist did, untold eons ago, so another scientist can do now. In the destruction of one Universe there can be the seed of another. And I shall create it!'

The sweep and the majesty of Martin's terrific ambition took Vola's breath away for the moment. Then she came to grips again with reality.

'You couldn't do it, Cran,' she said. 'You would have to be within the non-space-time in order to pass your thoughts into it, and the very fact of being within it would destroy you.'

'One doesn't have to be within it,' he answered. 'I should project my thoughts from a part of the Universe where normal laws still obtain . . . But to attempt such a mighty feat I would need intelligence such as I have not yet even attempted to acquire. I must become cleverer — and still cleverer, refining my mind, until I achieve absolute dearness of vision and can handle the huge elemental forces associated with the project.'

'It would be simpler to die,' Vola responded quietly, and Martin gazed at her fixedly.

'What kind of a woman are you?' he demanded. 'I offer you — and the rest of the race — a new Universe, new worlds which we alone will own, and you say it would be simpler to die! I just do not understand.'

'You are in no position to. You have become obsessed with your ambitions and the fact that you are a super-genius. You believe there is nothing you cannot do. But there is, Cran; there is!' Vola's eyes were gleaming with the intensity of her emotion. 'A super-scientist may have created the Universe which is now dying around us, but I believe as all natural people do, however scientific they may be — that that super-scientist must have been a God. Something beyond our ken. You cannot imitate such a scheme as that. It would annihilate you.'

Martin relaxed and smiled coldly. 'We shall see,' he said. 'I intend to experiment. You can either help me, or not, as you wish. And I do not want to hear any more remarks about a God creating a Universe. It savours of the lowliest primitive. Very unbecoming in a queen and a scientist.'

He turned away, intending to leave the terrace and re-enter the laboratory. Vola caught at his arm.

'Cran, what do you intend to do?' she asked anxiously.

'I intend to assemble a thought-amplifier in a space-machine and take it out to the very rim of that advancing Dark. I am going to project thoughts into the abyss and see what happens. If my theory is correct and matter forms as a result of my thoughts, then I shall return and make myself into the genius who can make a new Universe to take the place of the old.'

Without even a glance over his shoulder he returned into the laboratory and began to busy himself with the various instruments. Vola stood watching him for a time, aware of complete helplessness. She thought once of destroying the main magnetic unit of the seventh-octave machine and then thought better of it. It would be simple work for Martin to rebuild it, and she would only earn his profound contempt . . . Her trouble was that she could see, from her lesser pinnacle, just where he was heading. She believed — rightly or wrongly she did not know — that in his attempt to create life where there should be death he could only encompass his own destruction.

Sick at heart she returned to the suite where she and Martin, when he had the time, spent their hours together.

'For this I made him turn into a genius,' she whispered, sinking down into the cushions and gazing before her. 'I did it because I believed he could overcome the Black Terror, and what has come from it? He has explained the Black Terror but admits it defeats him. From which he passes on to the creation of a Universe . . . There has got to be an end to it. He must be stopped. Death in the natural orders would be so much simpler — and normal. If only there was a way to make him unlearn what he knows, return him to his previous state where these vast conceptions would never occur to him.'

She gave this problem considerable thought. Being herself an expert scientist she was able to examine the matter from every aspect, but in the end she was forced to the conclusion there was nothing she could do. To de-evolve Martin was quite impossible, any more than a tree could return to a sapling. Night arrived and the lights came up in the suite. She still wrestled with the problem. Then Martin came in silently and stood regarding her. There was upon his face that terrifying expression of cold authority.

'I did not find you very helpful in the laboratory, Vola,' he stated.

'I was tired, Cran. I came in to relax. We have been working very hard recently.'

To her surprise, he nodded slowly. 'Yes, I suppose we have. I am apt to forget at times that others have not my staying power . . . Fetch me some refreshment,' he snapped to a robot, then he came across to the cushions and settled at Vola's side.

'Have you built your projector? Your amplifier?'

'I started it — then abandoned it. I have come to the conclusion that you are correct.'

Relief suddenly came into Vola's face. She caught at Martin's shoulders tightly.

'Cran, look at me!' she entreated. 'I *am* correct: I know I am. It will never benefit you to create a Universe — '

'I was not referring to that,' he interrupted. 'My mind is made up on that score. I mean that you are correct in assuming thought-waves cannot influence a non-space-time if one is outside it. One must be within it.'

'Oh . . . But it is impossible to be in Nothing and create Something!'

'Aptly put,' Martin commented, musing. 'I made an experiment with a small amplifier and projected thought-waves. I find that when they pass through normal conditions, such as we have around us now, there is an intense diminution of power. They reach their destination with a loss of eighty per cent of their original efficiency. Obviously, then, one cannot project thought waves from the existing into the Non-Universe. They would have no strength when they arrived. So that is the problem I face. How to be within Nothing and create Something.'

'Forget it, Cran!' Vola insisted. 'I beg of you!'

The arrival of refreshment checked her for a while. Martin began to eat slowly, more as a duty than a necessity.

'It is certainly a problem,' he confessed at length. 'One that I cannot solve in my present state of intelligence. So the only solution to that is to become higher in the scale. I have to find the answer. I do not intend that our science and race shall be overwhelmed by a primal explosion. It is not befitting of intelligent beings. Your own fears, Vola, are purely born of ignorance. See it from my standpoint and you would realize I am right.'

'You wish that I should become a genius, too?' she asked quietly.

'Rather than you behave like a fool, yes.'

She met the cold challenge of his eyes and then shook her head.

'No, Cran. I will stay as I am. I have seen what forced evolution has done to you, and I certainly don't want any of it.'

'It was your suggestion in the first place. I was not at all keen on the idea. Now I have discovered how magnificent a thing it is to have knowledge I am anxious for more. In fact I have developed an insatiable thirst for it!'

Vola did not answer and for a while the refreshment was consumed in silence. Then Martin said:

'According to my calculations this world has six years to live — by Earth standards. When that period has elapsed the Dark will be upon us. The dissolution of all things and, when I have mastered the problem, the creation of a new Universe and its myriad worlds. All ours

— mine — to populate as we like. The product of my thoughts! Before I take the ultimate step that will carry me to the limit of evolution, however, I have other tests to make. I propose to send a thinking robot into the Dark and see what happens to him.'

'The robots *don't* think,' Vola reminded him wearily. 'All they do is obey the thought vibrations of their creators. We cannot create thoughts.'

'We can — and we shall. If not that, then I shall create a robot brain that will be in sympathy with the thought-sea around us, just as a natural brain is . . . That is my next move.' Martin got to his feet. 'If you wish to help me come to the laboratory.'

'Later,' Vola replied, thinking; so with a shrug Martin turned and left the huge chamber.

Vola remained lost in speculation for a long time, then at last she rose from the cushions and made her way through the airy spaces of the mighty building. She finished her journey at the suite of the Dispenser.

'Highness,' he greeted her gravely, as a robot opened the door for her. 'This is an honour.'

He motioned to a luxurious chair and Vola seated herself. Her face was drawn and serious.

'Dispenser, you are many years older than I,' she said quietly, 'and I have come to respect your judgment and wisdom. In the days when my father was alive your knowledge helped him over many a problem.'

The Dispenser smiled gravely. 'I was only too happy to assist your father, Highness. Am I to assume from your expression and general manner that some problem faces you?'

'Yes. Your ruler, my husband, is consumed with a scientific conception which I feel will bring about his destruction. I am partly to blame for it, even though I acted in the best interests of the race at the time. I believed, if he made himself a genius by seventh-octave radiation, he could overcome the Black Terror. Instead of that he admits defeat in that direction and instead wishes to create a Universe by projecting thought into non-space-time.'

'Scientifically, Highness, there is nothing illogical about that, although I cannot myself see how he proposes to do it.'

'I think he is venturing too far. I want to stop him. Already I have lost him as a husband. Only one thing can halt his crazy desire for more knowledge gained by evolution, and that is to stop him in his tracks, turn him back into the somewhat vague young man he used to be before he evolved. I can think of no way to do it: can you?'

The Dispenser brooded. 'Evolution is irreversible,' he said. 'He cannot unlearn what he knows. It is against all natural law. There is only one thing can stop him, and that I hesitate to name — '

'Don't hesitate, please. Be absolutely frank with me.'

'He must die, Highness, Nothing else can halt him ... But of course if you believe he will die in any case by trying to create a new Universe from his own thoughts, there is no point in that. You see, he might succeed in this grandiose scheme of his. If he did, it would be the supreme achievement.'

Vola's expression changed. 'What you really mean is, you think my fears are foolish?'

'No, Highness. I can understand your concern for your husband, and your distress at having lost him as a man, but the fact does remain that he is making an attempt to save us all from complete extinction. I think you should support him, not hinder his efforts.'

'Though all my woman's being cries out against it?'

'You refer to instinct, I suppose? You have the intuitive feeling that only disaster can result?'

Vola rose and began to move restlessly. 'I am convinced of it. That is why I am so afraid. I — ' She paused, an idea suddenly occurring to her. She asked a question slowly.

'What would happen, Dispenser, if his mind were disturbed? If, for instance, he tried to live two lives instead of one? You know by now, as all the city inhabitants do, of his twinship with a being on Earth, a faraway world, who either died or otherwise lost consciousness. Suppose that person is not dead? Suppose he could be revived? His consciousness coming back to life would be bound to throw my husband's mind off balance.'

'I imagine so . . . ' The Dispenser hesitated. 'But, Highness, if this other being is dead — '

'If he is, I can do nothing. If he is not, there may be some method with our science to revive him.' Vola looked up with suddenly brightened eyes. 'I know what I shall do! I shall travel to this faraway world and find Cran's twin. If he lives I shall restore him, make his mind active so, being linked to Cran's, it will upset his balance. In that way it is more than possible he will lose his genius and return to being a Sleeper. Better that than trying to duplicate Nature.'

'The decision rests with you, Highness,' the Dispenser responded, and he did not venture any further comment.

Not that Vola would have cared if he had. Her mind was made up and she had a plan that would keep her active. No matter how outlandish it seemed it was preferable to sitting around watching Martin furthering his own astounding schemes.

Vola wasted no time. She left a message on the recorder for Martin saying that she had gone on a short cruise to see if she could gain any information concerning the Black Terror; then half an hour later her space-machine, loaded with scientific equipment and full provisions, was flashing outwards into the void. From the stellar charts she knew the approximate position of the G-type dwarf star that was the sun of the planet Earth, but as yet it was not even visible. The distance from Hytro to Earth was colossal. Moving at the speed of light — 186,000 miles a second — it would take several years at least to cover the journey, and as many again to return.

But the space-machine did not limit itself to light-speed. Vola increased the velocity incessantly as the awful abysses of space loomed around her. Faster and faster yet, until finally the strange craft was flashing along the repulsive magnetic lines of force at over one and a half million miles a second. Even at this speed, it would be a desperately long trip — but Vola was prepared for it. She had no intention of immediately making the return journey. If she could only revive the twin of Cran, if he still lived, that would be enough. He would automatically establish his mental link with his twin almost instantly . . .

She began to realize, however, as time passed, that her machine was not behaving normally. All her efforts to build up even more speed resulted in failure. In fact she was losing velocity with a startling rapidity. The only reason could be some immense matter formation somewhere in the void, invisible perhaps, which was exerting its mass-attraction. She used her instruments to detect it and none of them registered. Then, just as she was about to give up the problem she noticed the magnetic compass at the rear of the vessel was pointing directly back through the void whence she had come.

Something, somewhere on Hytro, was exerting a terrific gravitational drag and pulling the machine back. And it was a something she could not defeat. There finally came a time when her vessel's advance had slowed to zero. This state reached, it began to move backwards with ever increasing speed, until at last it was hurtling on the return Journey to Hytro at stupendous velocity. Then, as Hytro was reached, her vessel was slowed, but still held fast. The machine landed quietly enough and, sullen-faced, Vola opened the airlock. Robots immediately came forward and seized her gently, but tightly. She was led, as though a captive, back to her own personal suite. Martin was waiting for her, his cadaverous face malignant.

'That was not very clever of you, Vola,' he said bitterly. 'I received your message and I certainly did not believe it. I had the astronomical section search space for you to see if you had really gone towards the Dark: instead, they discovered you hurtling into the outer depths. There could be only one place you were heading for in that direction — Earth. And I think I know why.'

Vola was silent. She realized now that Martin had acquired another gift. He was telepathic.

'Yes, I can read thoughts,' he said, as she pondered on this. 'Although you were so far away from me in space I could still read them. You hoped to go to Earth and revive my twin, using his awakened mind to upset mine. You fool! It would have taken you many months to reach Earth. Do you suppose that my twin could be *alive* after such a time? If he were, his thoughts would have affected me long ago. He is dead, Vola — quite dead, and because of it I am in possession of all my faculties. Henceforth, since you cannot support me as a wife and a queen should, I shall have you closely guarded.'

'I realize my mistake now, Cran,' Vola said, shrugging. 'It never occurred to me your twin *must* be dead. Naturally he would not just stay unconscious all this time.'

Martin motioned the robots away and came forward. He took hold of Vola's slim shoulders roughly.

'Vola, why do you distrust me so?' he demanded.

'Not you, Cran: just your plans. I believe you will destroy yourself by turning into a Creator.'

'You do not think I am such a fool as to risk being a Creator without making a test first, do you? I have completed the thinking robot during your absence, and I intend to try it out. I think you should see what it can do.'

'Very well.' Vola gave a sigh. All the fight had gone out of her.

She turned and followed Martin from the suite to the space-machine grounds, entering a machine in which there stood one of the medium-sized robots. The only difference about him was that his cranial-case was unusually large. Martin locked the sealing sheath over the door and then motioned to the automaton.

'He possesses an artificial brain patterned identically after my own,' he said. 'He also possesses a heart and bloodstream. In fact, physically, he is a reproduction of myself. I intend to travel to the nearest safe point outside the Black Terror and then project this robot into the Dark by means of force rays. A time switch will start his bloodstream and brain functioning after a while, which means he will operate as I would if I ventured into the Dark myself. I shall withdraw him and see what effect has been produced upon him. At the moment his artificial brain is storing up impressions from the surrounding thought-sea, as a battery stores current. When the time switch operates his thoughts will be radiated, and we shall see the effect on non-space-time.'

Vola nodded but she did not say anything. She had the secret hope that the robot might bring salvation by being so utterly destroyed in the Black Terror that Martin would think twice about his schemes.

Martin moved the controls and the space-machine began rising, rapidly increasing its velocity as it hurtled towards the Milky Way. Then it began to turn in the titanic arc, which brought it directly facing that incomprehensible Dark looming behind the more distant stars.

'We have a long journey,' Martin said, considering the void. 'We must rest, eat, and watch — in turn. I will stay on duty for the first period. You may as well retire.'

Vola did so; then she took over duty whilst Martin rested. So it went on as the terrific distance to the Black Terror was gradually lessened; until finally Martin decided that they were near enough, yet with enough margin for safety. He had to take into account that that black unknown was sweeping forward at stupendous speed and, if calculations were not exact, there was the chance of being overwhelmed by it.

By degrees the space-machine slackened speed, and continued to slacken through many hours of Earth-time, until finally it was comparatively motionless. Ahead were distant stars and, beyond them, the Everlasting Dark.

'Now we shall see,' Martin said, his eyes gleaming.

He picked up the robot and placed it in an ejection gun. He spent a moment or two reckoning out the initial thrust required to hurl the robot across the vast distance which would carry it at constant velocity straight into the Black Terror. This done, he released the switch and moved to the window. Vola, too, stood watching.

The robot shot out into space and was gone instantly, moving at incredible speed. Martin turned to the instruments and studied them, one particular needle speeding round its dial and showing by magnetic reaction from the travelling robot just where it was and how far it had got.

'Everything beautifully timed, Vola,' Martin said, glancing at her set, serious face. 'He will strike the Dark in about six hours from now. I set his mental time-switch for seven hours, so that allows him leeway. As to withdrawing him: that is simple. Magnetic attraction.'

'You believe he will come back?' Vola asked quietly.

'I am hoping so. If he does not the experiment may be considered a failure. If that should happen I have only one course — to venture into the Dark myself. Not now, but later, when I am possessed of the full power of my genius.'

Vola did not comment. She had already learned that it was useless to argue. She gazed out on the void for a while then, tiring of it, she retired to her bunk to rest. With hardly any exchange of words the six hours passed, Martin remaining at the instruments, ready for instant action.

'He has entered the Dark!' he exclaimed suddenly, and the tenseness in his tone brought Vola from her bunk to look at the instruments. She gave a frown as she studied them.

'Nothing is registering, Cran! They are all at zero.'

'I know.' His face was strained. 'I rather expected it. Since the robot is in non-space-time nothing can register, I suppose. It is an emptiness where everything is void and without form. The moment he crossed the rim into the Dark the instruments ceased operating . . . We have sixty minutes to go before his stored up thoughts are released into that unknown space.'

If time had dragged before it positively crawled now. Martin did not move from the instruments: he kept anxious eyes fixed upon them whilst Vola gazed through the window and out towards the stars. She did not know what she expected to see in that abysmal onrushing emptiness when the robot's thoughts were released. She felt there might be anything. A cosmic cataclysm, perhaps — The sixty minutes passed. Outside, space remained unchanged. On the instrument board there was not a flicker of reaction. Martin sat brooding. It was a long while before he spoke.

'There can be no doubt, if the robot remained in one piece, that thoughts *were* released from it,' he declared. 'But it does not seem to have had any effect on non-space-time. Why, I do not know, at my present level of intelligence. I must withdraw the robot and examine him.'

He closed the switches that operated the magnetic controls and there commenced another long, deadly wait. One hour — two — three. Six hours had to elapse before the robot should come back . . . But the robot did not come back. At the end of seven hours space was as empty as it had been at first. Vola smiled a little to herself, feeling that perhaps this total failure would cause Martin to revise his views.

Baffled, he rose from the control board and considered the void. He clenched a fist and beat it gently on the window frame.

'I don't understand it,' he declared. 'I just don't!'

'Because that non-space-time is something which only existed before the Universe was created,' Vola answered. 'You cannot be expected to understand that! Cran, why not admit you are beaten? Let us make preparations to die; or if not that then move our race elsewhere to a far distant world where at least we may have a little respite.'

'No,' he said quietly.

'But Cran — '

'No! I shall not allow this enigma to beat me. I am determined you, and I, and all our race shall continue to live in a Universe of my own devising. I must return home and acquire full genius in order that I may understand this problem.'

Plainly, his mind was made up. Without another word he returned to the switchboard, swung the machine round in an arc, and began to streak it back with ever mounting velocity to the remoteness where Hytro lay.

5

New Universe

Driven on by his insatiable lust for knowledge, and triumph over the deadly unknown that threatened, Martin wasted no time in placing himself in the area of the seventh-octave machine once he returned to Hytro. Vola, who had completely given up all hope of reasoning with him, was not present when he made his final effort to reach the ultimate of evolution. She retired to the suite, and there waited.

After a long interval Martin came to her. She was reclining on the silken cushions, finding relaxation and idleness the only sedative for her mental turmoil. For a moment she did not recognize the being who had entered.

He was far smaller than she — a shrunken mummy of a man, his few clothes hanging about him in bags.

Pipe-stem arms and legs, a scrawny neck, narrow chest and atrophied shoulders — and then the head. So enormous, so distended, so hairless, it looked like a bladder inflated to capacity. Upon its smoothness veins were pulsating.

'You — you are Cran?' Vola whispered, slowly rising and staring in horror.

The withered being halted within a few feet of her. His voice was reedy and cracked.

'Yes, I am Cran. I have covered the entire scale of evolution this time. I have gone as far as flesh and blood dare go. The next stage would have been a different fleshly vestment altogether — probably a bacterial form, the most advanced and indestructible type of life that can exist. You see in me, Vola, the men of our race as they will look countless cycles in the future. I do not say *if* they live that long, because they will. In the Universe I shall create . . . I know everything now, Vola, and it is a vast and over-powering responsibility.'

Martin came forward again and sank wearily on the cushions. Vola still looked at him in blank revulsion, her lithe body tensed ready to run away from him.

'You have nothing to fear, my dear,' he said at length. 'Emotion was already dead in the earlier form of myself: now it is totally extinct. I have all knowledge and a body so fragile, so wasted in feeding this colossal brain, that it is a burden to even possess it at all. With a slight effort I could will it out of existence and become disembodied thought — but that I will not do. I must have some kind of physical identity . . . I know now what happened to that robot. I have reasoned it out in the light of my present knowledge.'

'Well, what *did* happen to it?' Vola questioned.

'It released thoughts, but not concentration. Between the two there is an infinity of difference.'

Completely puzzled Vola made no response, but realizing this wizened being was only a travesty of the original Cran she plucked up courage and sat on the cushions near him.

'Thoughts, of themselves, are as useless as the wind to bend the walls of steel,'

Martin mused. 'But *concentration*, the battering, surging impact of thought waves, can create! All my robot did was disseminate a lot of useless, stored-up thought-waves into a non-space-time, which thoughts would have no possible reaction whatever. The robot then dissolved into nothing because no thing can exist where Time is not. It became a minus-quantity. Except . . . '

Vola waited. For a long time Martin meditated, his tiny eyes hidden under his enormous frontal forehead.

'Except that, by accident, I may have tossed into the Dark a duplicate of myself,' he finished. 'A duplicate which at present has no entity because nothing exists in that region.'

'A kind of dormant seed?' Vola suggested, trying to understand.

'One might call it that.' Martin turned his wizened face to look at her. 'That robot was patterned exactly after my image, both mentally and physically, the one difference being that he was artificial. His brain had the identical convolutions to mine and must have been in exact self-same sympathy with the thought-sea around us. Which means that when he dematerialized and his thoughts were scattered his mental entity remained. It must still be there, unclothed, asleep, waiting for something to stir on the face of the void. Where there is a brain, Vola, there is a mental entity. And nothing can destroy thought because it is a higher form than matter.'

Vola moved a little. 'Cran, do you realize something? You have two doubles now, or at least you would have had if the one on Earth were still living.'

Martin gave something approaching a smile. 'On Earth there is no double any more, Vola. The only other one is quiescent, in non-space-time. That quiescence will pass when I create the new Universe.'

'Then you still mean to do it?'

'Certainly. For that reason I evolved to the limit. I can do it now with assurance. I have every celestial and elemental fact within my grasp. I intend to leave now for the Black Terror and enter it. I shall bend it to my will.'

'Now?' Vola scrambled to her feet hurriedly. 'But, Cran, why? Would it not be better to wait until the Dark catches up with us? It would give us time to prepare.'

Martin rose, too, dominant despite his strange form.

'I require no time to prepare. Now, in the towering height of my genius, I must act.'

'But what of our race? You mean to desert them?'

'They are living units. As such they will be absorbed in the Universe I shall create, and will live again. Not perhaps in a form we shall recognize, but life will be there just the same. All those who are alive in the remaining Universe at the moment, Vola, will be absorbed into the new one I shall create. It will overtake and thrust aside this onrushing tide of the primal explosion. It will be overwhelmed by the greater expanding explosion from the primal core I shall create . . . And I intend to do it now.' Martin paused and then added, 'And you shall come with me.'

'No. No, Cran . . . I will not do it!' Vola

began to back away, but she did not go very far. Martin's eyes were fixed on hers and she began to feel the irresistible compulsion of his thoughts. She came to a halt.

'You will come with me, Vola, because you are my mate,' Martin stated flatly. 'I shall need you in the Universe which is to be.'

Vola had not the power any more to refuse. Turning, she followed Martin obediently from the room and, presently, to the hangar where the space-machines were housed. Thereafter everything was a daze to her as the vast journey through the void was made yet again towards the Black Terror. It was only when the machine was within a million miles of its nearest point of advance that Martin relaxed his iron mental grip.

'We are going straight ahead,' he said deliberately, as he rose from the control board. 'The machine is hurtling forward in a straight line and in a matter of minutes we shall enter that unknown region. When that happens I shall concentrate with all my power, which very concentration will prevent my dissolution, I trust. If that does not happen, then I shall become disembodied — but my thoughts will remain because nothing can destroy them. I shall dwell on only one fixed idea — the primal atom! From which a new Universe must come. It happened in the dim Beginning when a scientist's thought waves impinged on non-space-time. It can — and shall — happen again.'

'And what happens to *me*?' Vola asked, her voice only a whisper.

'Your mental entity will remain. Your body, I expect, will be destroyed. Have no fear. I shall always be present to protect you. I have not forgotten that you are my mate, low in the mental scale though you have become compared to me.'

Vola caught at his hands desperately. 'Cran, before you do this thing, think again! It will not work out as you believe. You are inflated with ego: you think you are the Artisan of the Universe Himself. There will — '

Vola could not finish. At that moment the onrushing space-machine flashed through the barrier into non-space-time. Instantly blank nothingness fell upon both Vola and Martin. It was the blankness born of the blasting and destruction of all physical attributes. Neither had bodies any more. Nothing was present except a sense of headlong motion. There was naught around except formless space-time, an endless wilderness without bounds, where no matter was. The primal dark, as it had existed before the Universe had come.

Since thought was no longer pinned by material encumbrances Martin suddenly realized that he was free. He thought of Vola, and the intense compulsion behind his wordless call brought her mental entity to him. Again he was dominant, and she subservient. She could only listen, a bemused, uncomprehending mentality.

'Free thoughts in free space!' came Martin's vibrations. 'Nothing to hold us! To us — to me — falls the enormous honour of creating a Universe! Think, Vola! That you *can* do! Concentrate! Interlocking thought vibrations must bring matter into being and create the primal atom!'

Convinced of his terrific authority and power Martin concentrated with all the scientific knowledge at his command. He could feel, too, the weaker impact of Vola's mind as she tried to help him. Before them something formed out of the greyness, fashioned by thought itself striking non-space-time.

It grew, expanded outwards, became the trembling primal atom of a new Universe! It exploded with bewildering force and created of itself mighty suns and nebulae.

The thought-entity that was Martin Clegg — Cran Zalto of Hytro — watched intently with omniscient eyes — then as the matter formed into the gradual birth of an expanding Universe a strange discovery startled him.

He was losing his memory! Like a drowning soul he could feel himself going down in the vast Universal cataclysm he had created. In his distress he cried out mentally to the only one who had ever tried to reason with him.

'Vola! Vola, where are you? Answer me!'

'I am here, Cran,' came her vibrations.

'Vola, something is wrong. Together we have created a Universe. We have fused thought into matter. When planets have cooled we would have gone to them, choosing one that suited us. We could have created a race of mighty scientists, you and I. But I am *forgetting*! Why? I do not understand!'

'It is this which I feared,' Vola answered. 'It is the reason why I tried so desperately to turn you from your inexorable purpose. We have created the Beginning, yes — but not the new Beginning as you had expected. Your thoughts and, in a weaker sense, mine formed this Universe — and that was only possible in non-space-time waiting for a disturbance to set it in motion. But now normal space-time has again been created and all its laws are operating. You and I are compelled to obey them. It is the eternal law, Cran. The upward climb which you and I made from the amoeba now counts for nothing. Oh, death would have been so much simpler! We might have stood a chance. Here we have none, for we have gone back to the core of the Beginning . . . You had forgotten *the* Creator!'

'Back?' Martin repeated. 'No! Not back to the very start after all I had achieved — No! No . . . '

His thoughts were a soundless scream on the face of the patterning void. Memory was vanishing like tape speeding from a reel. Every conception was being torn away. All his knowledge evaporating.

Down — down — down — In the endless abyss of his own creating.

★ ★ ★

Earth was in the throws of its birth. It resembled the interior of a blast furnace more than the outline of a planet. Centuries followed centuries: the years spread into the millions. Solidifying rock. Seas beneath the vapours. A moon slowly receding to become the monarch of the night. Clouds. Rain. The Deluge — and amidst it the first signs of life. Bacteria, then the lowly amoeba, progenitor of the human race.

Onwards to the Age of Fishes — the Carboniferous Age with its rioting vegetation. The Mesozoic period with its ground-shaking monsters and herbivorous reptiles.

The first birds, the first mammals, and then Pithecanthropus Erectus, the walking ape-man. Heidelberg Man — the 'Dawn Man' and his crude eolith. Neanderthal man, prototype of the real man. And at last the Cro-Magnon, first of the true men.

Such a being was Un-Wan, leader of his tribe. He was a leader because he was the mightiest hunter of all. None could slay the wild horse or bearded pony as quickly as he. Nor was the bison able to escape his spears and deadly accurate stones. Un-Wan was the master of his tribe, and of course the tribe was nomadic. But at the moment it was sheltering from the pitiless winter, deep in the caves where the lumbering mammoth could not reach.

Un-Wan had a mate, every whit as powerful — and as ugly — as himself. But there was something more than being just a hunter which made Un-Wan the leader of his tribe. He had, for his race, a commendable intelligence, and he certainly had imagination, a rare thing in a brain so undeveloped. He could tell a story, too, in a crude way, which always succeeded in holding his mate spellbound.

'Un-Wan dream of chariots in the sky,' he growled, in his thick, bestial voice. 'Un-Wan dream of other warriors. Men who use fire sticks for killing and who fly through the air in strange birds.'

'Of what does Un-Wan speak?' his mate asked, busy with the primitive fire and hot stones.

'Un-Wan dream,' the Cro-Magnon tribal leader insisted. 'In sleep Un-Wan is not Un-Wan any more. He is — somebody else. Faraway. So faraway.'

And whilst Un-Wan brooded over the mystery of his dreams, a higher form of man, who had developed more rapidly under the influence of the intense radiation of his larger sun, was also puzzled. He knew that, somewhere, in a place he could not identify, there existed an image of himself. He could not understand it. He put the problem to the more learned ones around him who were struggling to create a perfect civilization against the odds of climate and a particularly violent type of sun.

'That you might possess a twin somewhere in space is not impossible,' was the response of one of the scientists. 'But surely, son, it ranks as insignificant against the tasks we have to fulfill? Do you not realize what we are striving to create? We aim at perfection — nothing less. A state where our race can rest at last and say: we have achieved the ultimate.'

'That will take many generations,' commented the puzzled young man.

'What of it? It is the natural destiny of any race to achieve perfection, and you should be proud to be a member of that race.'

So the young man remained with his problem unanswered, and on an infinitely distant planet a Cro-Magnon man sat crouched beside his mate and peeped out upon the mystery of the heavens. Instinctively, animal-like, he knew there was something he ought to understand, but could not . . .

Throughout his life of danger and battle Un-Wan never solved the mystery of his dreams. He appealed to the witchdoctor of the tribe, but even his bewildering hocus-pocus brought no answer, or relief to the warrior's troubled mind. Nor could his mate help him, though she tried.

A similar battle proceeded in the mind of the young man, now grown much older, who struggled with his elders against the endless complications of producing a flawless civilization. On his own faraway world near a sun that blazed with an ever-deepening tinge of reddish orange, he tried to analyze the disturbances of his mind, and failed. Neither he, nor his race, were as yet scientific enough to grasp the mysteries of mind or understand the problems of inter-galactic space.

On Earth, Un-Wan fought his last battle and died before the merciless tusks of a mammoth — but his puzzled mind lived on, completely indestructible. The

Old Stone Age gave place to the New Stone Age — the Neolithic phase. The world was warmer now, plants and animals were being used for domestic purposes. The dim beginnings of a civilization, in the hands of the Grimaldis and the Azilians, were commencing to take shape. And at the head of one of the tribes was Vil-Kio, a man with an imagination. An imagination born chiefly of his amazing dreams wherein he believed he was another person. To the tribe he seemed god-like because of his beliefs and for this reason achieved as much eminence as the witchdoctors. But Val-Kio was deeply perplexed. He could not understand why he should have to live two lives simultaneously and neither could Han Velso, living on a world that had an orange-red star for a sun.

Han Velso was a scientist, one of the leaders in the construction of a perfect civilization. Generations had passed and still the ultimate perfection had not been achieved.

One day Han Velso found himself taken to task by one of the elders of the master-city. In fact the interrogator was more than an elder: he was the ruler of the planet.

'Han there is much about your behaviour which I am at a loss to understand,' the ruler commented, musing. 'You are a good scientist, and you help us with our monumental task of creating perfection for the masses — yet you seem to do it from a sense of duty rather than from an urge of the heart. What's the matter with you?'

'Nothing, Excellency,' the young man responded, a trifle uncomfortably.

'That I find it hard to believe. You are always thinking of something apart from your immediate task. Everybody has noticed it, and there must he a reason. Have you consulted the mind experts?'

'I have, Excellency, and they cannot explain it. I doubt if even you, in your wisdom, would understand it.'

'I have solved many intricate problems,' the ruler responded gravely.

'This one is different, Excellency. I believe I am two people simultaneously.'

'That is impossible. You were born as a

single unit. You had no twin.'

'I know. That is what makes it so baffling. I do not believe this other self exists on this world at all, but somewhere very far away. On another planet in the depths of space ... I have searched through our records, and I find that in this instance I am not unique. A predecessor of mine, one who was in this vast scientific army creating this perfect civilization, also suffered from the same distraction or delusion, or whatever it is.'

'To whom do you refer?'

'His name was Mir Landoz. He lived generations ago when our world was much younger and our perfect civilization only just in its incipiency.'

'Yes, I have read of him,' the ruler admitted. 'It can hardly have any connection with you, can it?'

'Only in that he suffered from the same strange mental disturbance. If one is to believe that the mind endures and reappears in different bodily forms after the transition of death, I think it possible I may be Mir Landoz, living again.'

'A large assumption,' the ruler commented dryly.

'But not beyond possibility, Excellency. I am scientist enough to know that.'

'Assuming you are right, it can hardly affect the present position. What I wish to know is: why do you allow this mental disturbance you speak of to influence your life? You work without heart; you ignore the presence of the woman to whom you are betrothed by the order of the State; you — '

'I just can't help it,' Han Velso interrupted. 'I am always at a mental loss, not sure whether I am myself — or somebody else.'

'Then it is time you rid yourself of such a preposterous delusion!' The ruler rose to his feet in anger. 'You seem to have forgotten that, in course of time, after many generations, your children's children might well become rulers of this planet. Suppose you transmit your so-called peculiarity to them? What kind of rulers do you think they would make?'

'I do not believe the condition can *be* transmitted, Excellency. It will, though, probably repeat itself somewhere long after I am dead — maybe in a body that will yet again be mine. I believe, unlike you, that we never really die — or at least that our minds do not. I believe thought to be indestructible and that on death only the material structure is destroyed. The mind reforms a fresh entity and assumes control when a material form is born in the normal way.'

'Your views are considerably ahead of your time,' the ruler snapped. 'For the moment I would be glad if you would confine yourself solely to assisting us in achieving perfection. There is a great deal to be done and it may yet be many generations before we provide for all our peoples he ultimate of comfort to which they are entitled.'

Han Velso was silent for a moment, convinced of the rightness of his argument, but powerless to enforce it against the ruler. So he turned and retired with dignity, closing the door.

And on faraway Earth Val-Kio ran his allotted span, and died. But in the generations that followed there were other men as dominant, and as perplexed, as he had been. The Neolithic phase passed. Civilization began to assume its crude first forms, an advance which could only be measured by the thousands of years. But once it started its upward climb it developed rapidly. The Sumerian and Egyptian civilization began to mature, and developing from them, in the land of Mu, came Atlantis. Atlantis had become the peak of achievement. Man had climbed a long way from his primal slime.

Atlantis lay between two continents, upon a vast tableland with the name of Mu. It represented the quintessence of the arts and sciences, the epitome of all that was best in the mighty Egyptian and Sumerian races. At its head was Dexos, and he was a man with a problem. He believed he was living two lives at once, and for all his knowledge and the scientific power grouped about him, he was not able to find an answer to the riddle. Even Efrina, his queen, though outstanding in scientific achievement, had no answer to give.

'It clouds my judgment, Efrina,' he

confessed one evening when they were together on the palace terrace basking in the heat of the descending sun. 'I believe this city of ours could achieve much more if I did not feel I was linked to some unexplained being so very far away.'

Efrina, blonde, aristocratic as became her heritage, was silent for a moment; then she asked a question.

'If you believe this unknown somebody is somewhere in space why do you not set out to find him?'

'Because, as near as my mentality can tell me, he exists at so great a distance our space travel could not reach him in the course of one lifetime. In fact many, many lifetimes would have to pass. If I had eternality, or we had space travel infinitely faster than the rocket principle, I would most certainly try and reach him.'

'Where do you imagine he is?'

'I think,' Dexos mused, 'he exists somewhere in the region of the variable stars. I suppose it must be as difficult for him as it is for me to maintain a steady concentration when disturbed by the thoughts of another. I often wonder does he feel as I do?'

Dexos glanced up as a messenger came out onto the terrace. His very urgency revealed that something unexpected had happened.

'Excellency, I think you had better come at once ... ' The man was breathing hard. 'Our astronomers believe something of extreme danger is approaching from the void. It may cause considerable havoc.'

'Oh?' Dexos looked puzzled for a moment, then he glanced at the girl. 'You had better come with me Efrina.'

They left the terrace together and passed through the royal suite into the corridor contiguous to it. Before long they were in the astronomical observatory where there was assembled the finest instruments Atlantean science could devise. A worried astronomer glanced up.

'Excellencies,' he greeted, with an obeisance, and then he hurried immediately into the reason for his anxiety. 'I have just noticed perturbations in the behavior of the outer planets: they are being influenced by something as yet

135

invisible approaching from the depths of space.'

'Invisible?' Dexos repeated. 'But surely that is unusual?'

'I believe it to be a form of extremely dark matter which fails to catch the light of the sun. These instruments show for themselves the tremendous disturbances taking place.'

Dexos and Efrina studied them for a while, their faces becoming grim as they saw the wild behavior of the needles. Definitely something of extreme mass-attraction was approaching.

'Apparently it is coming this way,' the astronomer continued in agitation. 'It will, of course, be drawn by the pull of the sun and possibly fall into it. That in itself, a solar collision, could produce havoc enough — but long before that takes place Earth will be subject to tremendous swings and shifts which may well bring everything down round our ears.'

'We must discover the nature of this something,' Dexos snapped. 'Send out space pilots immediately to gather all the facts they can.'

His orders were obeyed and within half an hour the most expert pilots of the city were winging their way into space, their machines equipped with all the necessary instruments for detecting the unknown something. Out of the six machines which set forth, only one returned. The others had been caught in the enormously powerful field of the approaching object and drawn to it, to crash to destruction.

The pilot and navigator who managed to survive brought back all the necessary detail, however, and Dexos and Efrina examined it without delay. Their conclusions were not very cheering.

'The approaching asteroid — for it is hardly more in size — is neutronium,' Dexos declared finally. 'Matter such as makes up some of the white dwarf suns, enormously compact, all the electrons stripped and only the nuclei left. In such a state even a small fragment of the substance can weigh many tons. Small though it is it has a tremendous mass weight, as large as that of Jupiter. Where it has come from we do not know: it is one of those interstellar wanderers who, by misfortune, is destined to pass through our solar system.'

'But it will mean chaos!' Efrina cried in horror.

'Yes. Chaos.' Dexos was silent for a while, drumming his fingertips on the bench. 'It is moving so rapidly that within seven more days it will be here. It hardly gives us time to prepare. We cannot destroy it. It seems to me that not only our city of Atlantis, but every civilized city on the planet, will be laid waste ... We must make our plans instantly. We have not a moment to lose.'

Within ten minutes he was broadcasting his information to the entire planet, and in its various civilized regions men and women moved like ants to make their preparations. Some travelled underground in the hope they might escape; others prepared scientific means of propping up their cities. Dexos was none too sure of either of these devices, and said so, summoning the Governing Council of Atlantis to hear him.

'Our only way to escape from Chaos, as we will name him, is to fly outwards into space,' he said. 'By outwards, I mean away from Chaos towards the sun. It is inevitable that the sun will claim him, which will mean he will not pursue us beyond that point. When the upheavals have subsided we will return and see what can be done — or else we will domicile ourselves on another world.'

'And leave all our magnificent scientific machines, all this master-civilization we have built up?' Efrina questioned.

'There can be no other way, Efrina. We have not the time to dismantle anything.'

'We have not, true, but is there any reason why we cannot construct living robots, imaged after ourselves, who can perhaps operate defensive mechanisms to save the equipment after we have gone?'

The Council waited for the girl to elaborate her idea. She commenced doing so.

'We have disintegrators and force shields,' she explained. 'With those, falling masonry and tumbling landscape can be repelled, thereby preventing our machinery from being damaged. For us to stay personally and control such equipment would be too dangerous, but robots patterned after us — thereby having the exact physical makeup, such as hands, arms, feet, and so forth, could perhaps save much. Their artificial brains could have the necessary orders and — '

'Yes, it is a useful notion,' Dexos interrupted, in quick agreement. 'I do not think they will be able to save much but at least it is worth trying. You and I will have robots made after our images immediately, and the necessary instructions can be recorded on their artificial brains. Come . . . '

6

The End of Atlantis

Within two hours the flesh and blood images of Dexos and Efrina were complete, synthetic to the last detail, and having duplication in everything except brains. These latter were made up of electronic components, which would react to the stored instructions that Dexos and Efrina then proceeded to give.

Not only were these two robots made, but others as well, to guard if possible all the valuable portions of the mighty city. This done there was no other course but to prepare for exodus — and then it was that the serious miscalculations of the pilot who had been into space became apparent. Possibly he was not to blame; possibly his instruments had been unduly influenced by the neutronium mass. Whatever the explanation the unseen but extremely powerful foreign body entered

141

the System many days ahead of time.

The first evidences of its devilish power to upset equilibrium became apparent when an earthquake of unexpected severity rippled across the globe. Dexos was in the huge roofless space where the rocket projectiles were being prepared for departure when the thing happened. With him was Efrina. They looked about them in surprise as the deep rumbling fell upon their ears. Then the floor began to quake and with a rattling concussion immense fissures opened in the walls.

'Dexos!' Efrina screamed in horror, as the top of the wall nearest him began to break in two. 'Dexos! Quickly — !'

He made a frantic effort to dash away from the falling metal, but he was seconds too late. It caught him edgewise and knocked him spinning a dozen yards, the top of his head completely crushed.

Efrina gazed after him with brimming eyes but before she could make any attempt to rush to him there came the second earthquake. Its violence was so tremendous Efrina found herself lifted and flung through the air. Throwing out a hand to save herself she caught hold of one of the projecting tubes on the nearby space-machine, and it steadied her . . . Dimly she realized that this was the beginning of the end. The earthquake shocks were becoming more violent with every moment. She could picture the city crumbling under the impact, an onslaught growing worse with every second as Chaos pervaded space with his abnormal mass.

There was one chance of survival, and Efrina took it. She dragged herself through the machine's airlock and stumbled into the control room, slamming the door. Quickly she gave the power to the jets and the machine lifted, hurtling into space. Moving to the window she looked down in horror upon utter destruction.

In all directions Atlantis was breaking up, the continent on which it stood rending in twain before the disturbance in balance. The sea was boiling and foaming inwards. In the distances mountains were levelling continents on the move. And the perturbations were affecting her space-machine, too. She realized it in time and changed her course so that she hurtled sunward ahead of the advancing heavy asteroid, and having reacted to the situation in time she succeeded in dragging her vessel free.

Whether others of the race had escaped in space-machines she did not know. Certainly Atlantis was doomed, and not even the robots would be able to save anything since they had been timed to operate for a period much later than this. They would be destroyed in the ruins of the civilization being submerged under the thundering oceans.

But Efrina had overlooked the fact that bodies float, and the synthetic doubles were no exception. When the laboratory fell to pieces about them they rose to the surface of the tumbling ocean. The image of Efrina survived, but not that of Dexos. Caught between floating trees it was crushed and pounded into pulp. So Efrina's image floated on alone, its brainpan waterlogged and useless, but its physical form still unimpaired. When the day came for the intricate components that had become waterlogged to dry out, it was conceivable that Efrina the Second might come to life, an exact image of her pattern.

For Efrina such considerations meant nothing. She was conscious of the fact that she was virtually alone in space, a woman without a world and without a fellow member of her race. For all she knew everything on the planet she had left behind had been destroyed.

She travelled far beyond the influence of the sun, and beyond the power of Chaos to reach her; and then she began a slow return. Or at least this was her intention. Instead she found herself assailed by an intense sleepiness, which constantly bothered her as she tried to make her calculations for the course. She had turned the vessel round and was heading back for Earth when the sleepiness became a positive thing bordering on unconsciousness.

Though her brain was blurred she realized what had happened. In her desperate dash from Earth she had overlooked everything except escaping — had forgotten the radiation-shields with which the vessel should have been covered. Passing so near the sun she had absorbed many of his extremely lethal radiations and now it was too late to do anything about it. Her body was riddled with the effects. She might fall into coma; she might die; she might only become motionless, her brain still alive and her body senseless.

She fell to the floor, her legs no longer able to support her. There she remained, her mind still active but unable to stir even a muscle to obey her bidding. It seemed that she had fallen prey to the violent radiation of the sun's photosphere, which had the power to slow the bodily functions to such a crawl that they were literally at a standstill. Such effects had been duplicated on animals in the laboratory. That meant that she was living at a fraction of normal speed even though her mind was normal. For all practical purposes she was possessed of a life of eternality and yet could not move. The ship hurtled on through free space, unimpeded. An incredible distance away there loomed Betelgeuse, gleaming with his orange-red fire.

Upon one of the seven worlds circling around Betelgeuse the ruler of the planet was addressing his peoples. He spoke from the peaceful sanctuary of his private chamber, his voice carried by radio waves to all parts of the planet.

'My friends, this is a great day in our lives,' he announced. 'After centuries of unremitting toil we have at last succeeded in creating the perfect civilization. It means that henceforth you, and those of you who have little to do in the essential services — which must be maintained — may live your lives in perfect peace. A dream-state if you will. Robots will take care of your every emotion. By this means your lives will be extended by hundreds of years because you will have no energy expended in the normal course of living.'

Amongst those who could be considered the youngest of the royal clique a young man listened. Until very recently he had suffered from the same complaint as one of his predecessors — the curious mental conviction that he was living in two places at once. But that strange belief had gone now — why he did not know — and for the first time in his life he felt the absolute master of himself. If there *had* been a twin somewhere it had ceased to influence him. He thought of the perfect peace the robots could provide. He thought of the woman whom he was to marry. In hundreds of years he might become the ruler of this race, not because of ability but by right of succession.

And in the Earth solar system the wandering mass of neutronium had ended its wild career and plunged into the sun. For a while that vast body had spewed forth deadly radiations and electronic streams, to finally settle down as the heavy mass was digested into the atomic maw. The worlds in the system found new balance. Survivors of the great catastrophe wandered about on the planets Earth, Mars, and Venus.

On Earth in particular man looked out fearfully on clearing heavens. The hell that had gone had left blasted minds and utterly annihilated civilizations. Where Atlantis had stood there was naught but rolling waters. Where the proud cities of the Egyptian dynasty had spread there was only the everlasting sand, the Sphinx and Pyramids alone undestroyed in the cataclysm.

Man was climbing again, with only the one advantage that he was not back to the stage of the amoeba. He was at least a man, though one no longer with education or knowledge. Only the healing work of peaceful centuries would be able to restore the balance essential for progress.

Amidst the teeming millions who moved back and forth over the Earth, seeking the best place to live, was a woman who was not really a woman at all. In appearance she exactly resembled the vanished Efrina of Atlantis. Since there were no doctors and surgery was a forgotten art, she was not aware that her brain was only a mass of electronic components created by brilliant scientists gone forever. In all other things she was a normal woman, and believed herself such. She had no more idea how she had been born than anybody else would have. That she had no records of her family was taken as normal after such an upheaval.

The last thing she knew was that, at a given period, time switches had operated and brought her to life in the midst of confusion.

She remembered something about machines she was supposed to guard, but since there were none the silent injunction, insistent at first, soon faded and expired. She married a fellow wanderer. She had children. The females resembled her in many ways. The family stemmed out . . .

And it was during the course of such generations that a lonely space machine continued its uninterrupted journey across the void. So free was space once the Earth system had been traversed there was no large mass to swing the tiny flier aside. On and on and on, with a motionless woman on the floor of its control room. Her mind still lived, nearly unbalanced by the endless years of relentless immovability. Her body, though it required scant sustenance because of its lack of movement, was none the less showing signs of wastage . . .

Until there came a time when at last the vessel was swung aside in its hurtling onrush. Efrina prayed for death to release her from her terrible prison. She fully expected that the machine would crash and that everything would go out in one bewildering blaze of disintegration. But in this she was mistaken. The ever-watchful scientists in the astronomical laboratories of the planet Hytro had seen the vessel's approach to their system. For them to inform the ruling retinue would have been a waste of time: all of them, including the ruler, were imbibing the induced comforts at the hands of the robots.

Force rays reached out into the void and caught the flyer in their grip. It was brought down gently instead of with overwhelming concussion and promptly removed to the hangars where it could be investigated. The motionless woman on the control-room floor, a woman attired in garments that stamped her as of high rank, was removed immediately to the surgical laboratories for examination.

Gradually Efrina came out of the abyss of near-death to the awareness of voices around her. She opened her eyes and looked on kindly faces, some of them rugged with age and the wisdom it brings.

A voice spoke. Efrina shook her head tiredly as she lay on a soft airbed. She could not understand the language. So robots were summoned who operated instruments containing long electrodes. Under their influence Efrina's brain cells were supplied with a complete knowledge of the principal tongue of Hytro.

'Whence came you?' asked the most rugged onlooker of all, smiling in welcome.

'From infinitely far,' Efrina answered warily. 'So far it is lost in time and memory. Many lifetimes. I was stricken down by photospheric radiation from my System's sun and lay motionless throughout the ages whilst my ship hurtled on — and on — and on.'

'None the less, you must have come from a world,' the craggy-faced one insisted. 'You are not unlike us in physical development, though somewhat smaller. Tell us all you can remember — and have no fear. You are amongst friends.'

By degrees Efrina told her story and

the scientists listened with profound attention. When it was over they glanced at one another, and then back to her.

'You have survived a tremendous ordeal, Queen Efrina, and we are glad to welcome you to our own civilization. If you wish, you can become a Dreamer, as most royal people do.'

'Dreamer?' Efrina repeated — but at that moment the process of induced life and its attendant emotions was not explained to her. She was instructed to rest.

Some days later her strength had returned. Surgery of the nth degree had brought her back almost to the point of youth and beauty she had achieved on Earth before the Catastrophe. Now she was one of the royal household of Hytro, but knowing inwardly she was different from these beings who preferred to spend their time on silken cushions, dreaming the hours away. The only person she could question was the kindly chief surgeon who had brought her back from near-extinction.

'I could never do as these people do,

Master,' she said quietly, as she and the surgeon talked on the terrace outside the royal suite. 'I prefer to live my life, not dream it. Whether that is a sin or not I cannot say.'

'No, my dear, it is not a sin,' the surgeon responded. 'There are many on the planet — men and women — who find a life of perfect ease too monotonous to follow. With you, born of another world, the emotion is quite understandable. My suggestion is that you should mate with one of the many worthy males of this race — those who still believe there is much to be done to make our planet perfect.'

'Pioneers?' Efrina questioned, thinking.

'One might call them that, yes. Up to now perfection for the body has been our aim — but there is still perfection of the planet itself to be attained. The inner mysteries of the sub-atomic world, gravitation, the precise meaning of force, and so on. All those things have yet to be mastered. Since our science is different from yours I do not see that you can do better than wed a scientist who can teach

154

you all you may wish to know . . . '

Efrina obeyed the suggestion some months later and married one of the most high-ranking young scientists on the planet. There was even a chance he, or at least his descendants, might become rulers one day. Many lifetimes later, perhaps, when all that could be done had been done . . .

The years passed on. To Efrina they were rich in experience and happiness. Her husband was all she could desire: her many children were as anxious to progress as were their parents. And on Earth the era of Christendom had commenced and advanced two centuries and more and the Roman Empire had risen and declined. Great names and mighty conquerors swept across the Earth scheme of things as the survivors of the Catastrophe fought upwards again on the ladder of evolution . . .

Ghengis Khan — Frederick the Great — Ivan the Terrible. Earth and Hytro, moving side by side, fashioned by time and yet parted by the inconceivable distances of interstellar space. On Earth

155

there was always a male somewhere in the teeming millions who believed he had a twin and, for that reason, found his mental clarity perpetually clouded. On Hytro the same condition existed, sometimes in a commoner, sometimes in one of royal rank. On Earth, at the close of the twentieth century, it was a worry that beset one Martin Clegg, who at the age of fifteen had begun to realize he was not as other boys. For him there were no peaceful nights. Always he dreamed of being somebody else, always he glimpsed far and mystifying horizons.

His parents had no patience with him. In fact, when they discovered that his peculiar mental aberration produced a very bad school report they flew into a rage. The following year Martin was yanked from school and bundled into an office to learn to be a draughtsman. Just about the same time that young Cran Zalto of Hytro was being given a supreme choice in connection with his future. Though still only sixteen there had fallen to Cran Zalto the onus of ruler. He stood and faced the Elders of the planet in the

Council Room and waited respectfully for what they might have to say.

'To you, Cran Zalto, at your young age, there falls the duty of ruler,' said the leader of the Elders. 'Your father was a man who believed in working to add perfection to a civilization already perfect. You cannot be expected to take on where he left off, but at least you are at an age to express whether you will wish to do so when you attain your majority.'

'I shall never have the wish to do so,' the youth answered, and the Elders glanced at one another in surprise.

'And why not?' demanded the leader. 'When your majority is reached you will be wed by law to Princess Vola and, together, you will direct the destinies of this planet. Her Highness comes from royal and pioneering stock which can be traced as far back as one Queen Efrina who, though an alien to our world, became as useful and attached to it as though she had been born here.'

'I know exactly what has been planned for me because I have been informed of it often enough,' Cran answered. 'But though I shall marry, as ordered, I have no intention of living the gruelling life of my father. He died prematurely from overwork. I prefer the happy stimulus of the Dreamers.'

'You, a king-to-be, prefer *that*?' cried the leader, aghast.

'Yes — but not entirely from my own choosing. I am mentally incapable of concentrating for any length of time upon any subject. My life is partly somebody else's — a being far away whom I find it difficult to comprehend.'

'There have been others in the race like this,' one of the Elders murmured to the leader. 'It is, I believe, some kind of mental disease, and there seems to be no cure for it. Let him have his way.'

'So be it,' the leader said, sighing. 'If it is your choice to become a Dreamer, we have no power to stop you. But I would warn you that you will not find the Princess Vola willing to join you in your life of blind mental luxury.'

'I did not choose the Princess Vola as my wife,' Cran replied, shrugging. 'If my tastes do not coincide with hers, none are to blame for that except the Elders . . . '

And, when he became of age in five more years, Cran Zalto did exactly as he had forecast. He married the blonde-headed Vola and ignored all her entreaties when he insisted that he must become a Dreamer.

'But why? *Why?*' she insisted, when, after the ceremony performed by the Dispenser, they were in their suite together. 'What is your reason? Is it that I am wholly undesirable?'

'You have nothing to do with it, Vola.' Cran paced up and down restlessly. 'In fact, were I a man of the type you obviously expect I would consider you a wife in a million. Rather than be a disappointment to you by trying to concentrate and improve our already perfect world, I prefer to retire to the artificial stimuli provided by the robots.'

'But there is so much to do!' Vola protested. 'Our parents devised this union of ours for that very reason. In the scientific field we have much to discover. We must also learn why it is we keep being invaded from outer space. It cannot be because our world is so delectable. Other worlds must be infinitely advanced on ours. Remember, there have already been two small invasions: there may be others. To even discover a reason for those is better than becoming a being who is dead and yet alive.'

Cran was silent, gazing out into the distances of the huge city through the open window. There was a warm breeze blowing. Just for a moment he was pervaded by the thought that he had been in this exactly identical situation before somewhere; then it was gone. Back of his mind was the consciousness of another mind moving. A being — somewhere — far away.

'Did you not hear me, Cran?' Vola demanded, her anxiety giving place to anger.

He turned, insolent in the firmness of his decision.

'I heard, Vola, yes — but my mind is made up.'

'But it is without all reason!' Vola complained, her tawny eyes fixed upon him. 'At least explain why you do not think you would be a success in — '

'There is a reason you would not understand, and I prefer not to discuss it. If you will forgive me, Vola, I intend to retire immediately to the Hall of Dreamers.'

And without another word Cran left the chamber, the girl gazing after him in puzzled amazement.

She was every bit as puzzled, in fact, as Martin Clegg. At almost this very moment in the scheme of things he was leaving the office where he worked as draughtsman and sauntering homewards through the summer dusk. He had no real reason for following the rough road that ran at the edge of Ridley's Common at the rear of the provincial town. It took him far out of his way — and yet he followed it every evening to his rooms. He liked its expanses. He had an opportunity to think, to perhaps still the chaotic disturbances in his mind. And also, when the weather was good, he had a chance to look at the sky and behold Orion stealing out of the paleness.

Orion. Betelgeuse. Why did they fascinate him so? What had he in common with something up there? He still insisted he had twinship, but now he had to insist it to himself. Everybody else laughed at him, and his parents died — prematurely — with the conviction that they had given to the world one who, if not mentally deficient, was decidedly 'strange.'

Martin Clegg, aged twenty-five, felt very much alone on this particular evening. As usual his troubled mind had made a mess of his work as a draughtsman. He might even get the sack before long. He settled down on a seat in the drowsy gloaming of the June night. It had been an exceptionally busy time at the office. Overtime had kept him late. But at least it had meant he could be out here in the fast coming dark and —

A thud disturbed him. A girl was hurrying past in the twilight, graceful in her summer frock, her blonde hair flowing in the light breeze. She had dropped her handbag on the concrete path. Before she could stoop Martin had retrieved it for her. Smiling in the twilight he handed it to her.

'Thank you,' she said demurely, and began to examine the clasp. Whether it was because the clasp was damaged or she was subtly feminine Martin Clegg did not know. He spoke in sudden concern.

'Oh, please — allow me. More of a man's job to fiddle with catches, you know.'

'You are very kind,' the girl murmured, and watched him peer at the clasp in the dim light. Finally, discovering some trifling fault, he returned to the seat and ignited his lighter. The flame was motionless in the windless, gnat-ridden air. The girl seated herself close beside him and waited.

In between performing mysterious feats of repair to the catch Martin took care to observe what the girl was like. Her hair was blonde; that much he knew. She seemed to have blue eyes in the lighter flame, and quite a pretty face. Good figure, too, and trim legs and feet. In fact Martin began to bless the inventor of handbags and the inexorable laws of gravity that had made the bag fall.

'There!' Martin exclaimed finally, realizing he could not play around indefinitely. 'I think you'll find that all right.'

'Thanks so much.' The girl took the

bag and half rose. Martin began to rise, then sat down again as she did.

'Remarkably still,' he said, and sounded very mid-Victorian.

'Yes. Probably a storm later.'

'Oh, I don't know. There is a slight breeze now and again. I noticed how it — er — caught your hair a moment or two ago.'

'You did?' The girl laughed musically. 'I find my hair a nuisance, really. Tumbles all over the place.'

Martin laughed, too, and then there was silence again. The stars came out mistily and the darkness deepened. With it the first chill began to settle.

'I really must be going,' the girl decided, rising definitely this time. 'My parents will be wondering. I said I was only going for a short stroll.'

'Perhaps I might accompany you home? The Common isn't always a safe place for a nice girl to be when darkness comes.'

'That's very considerate of you, Mr. — er — '

'The name's Martin Clegg.'

'I'm Elsie Barlow. Now I suppose we

ought to shake hands?'

Martin laughed and as they walked they clasped hands firmly and talked of cabbages and kings. Throughout his life Martin had never been sure of himself because he had been ruled by that Other, so far away, but of one thing this night he was sure. Elsie Barlow had come into his life and was going to remain in it. On that he was determined.

He saw her to her home, learned that she worked in a local office, that her parents were genial, happy-go-lucky people, and that she liked dancing, films, and good books. He also gathered obliquely that she was three years his junior. This being a good total for the first night he left her with the promise that they would meet the following evening — and spend it at the Apex Cinema. For perhaps the first time in his life Martin was really happy. Even the cloudy dominance of the Other did not obsess him as much as usual —

Until he reached home, or at least his rooms. Retiring to bed he began again that mad rambling through chaotic dreams wherein he was a person who ruled a race, a race so perfect he could not understand it. Elsie Barlow was mixed up in it somewhere, too, only now she looked like a Grecian, flowing robes of white, her corn-colored hair held in position at the crown of her head with a golden band. She was moving swiftly down a corridor which seemed of interminable length — Then the vision faded and Martin tossed uneasily. He seemed to hear a voice, just like Elsie Barlow's, calling across the tumbled confusion of his mind.

'Cran! Cran Zalto! Wake up! Come immediately! It is most urgent!'

Vola stood looking at Cran as she spoke to him, her delicate hand shaking his shoulder. He stirred in drowsy comfort amidst the cushions and the robots floated gently around him, moving the electrodes with which they were emotionally feeding him.

'Fool! Dreaming, useless fool!' Vola cried hoarsely, then in agitation she turned and hurried from the great hall sweeping aside the robots who came gliding to her assistance. She finished her journey in the suite of the Dispenser.

'Highness!' he exclaimed in surprise, rising, 'you seem distraught.'

'I am,' she retorted, her face set. 'I have just received information that another invasion is headed for this planet of ours and I cannot stir my husband to action. What am I to do, Dispenser? The danger is imminent. You can delegate my husband's powers to me and let me give the orders to save us . . . '

'No, Highness, I am bound by law to respect your husband's higher authority — '

'But he dreams — and dreams — and dreams, soaking in the perfection created by his ancestors!'

'And yours, Highness.'

Vola shrugged. 'I am called a Retrograde because I will not participate in this living-death of the Hall of Dreamers. That does not worry, me. I come from a line of pioneers and fighters and that is why I wish to smash the challenge of this approaching armada.'

The Dispenser thought swiftly, then he

said, 'In such an emergency as this power must automatically move to the next in authority — which is your Highness. Very well, do as you wish, and I will give my sanction publicly.'

Vola's eyes were bright with gratitude. She hurried quickly from the suite and finally reached the enormous central laboratory. Here there were flesh and blood as well as robot technicians at work — but work ceased at her command.

'Direct all your energies to the remote control apparatus,' she instructed. 'Switch on the defensive screens and operate them as dictated by the observatory technicians. They are watching space and the armada headed this way. If possible I require prisoners for questioning. I wish to learn why these invasions constantly take place. I delegate you two to fetch me a prisoner.'

Immediately the two robots she had singled out began to move, and with blind obedience they entered a space-machine and set out to fulfill the commands of their mistress if at all possible.

Meanwhile, the terrifying defensive

power of Hytro opened up by remote control, every sector of the action controlled by men or robots sitting impassively at their switchboards, moving the keys on the consoles which rained destruction at the in-sweeping armada.

There were disruptive screens, gigantic atomic force guns, barrages of vibration. The unknown invaders retaliated with weapons that proved they were as scientific as their adversaries, hurtling walls of shattering vibration down upon the defenses. But they could not break the remote control onslaught that persistently smashed into them. Gradually their ascendancy was broken and the danger passed.

Four hours after the battle had ended, with strewn hulks of wrecked space-machines lying in various parts of Hytro, a prisoner was brought into the laboratory by the two robots and placed before Vola. She eyed him in cold hostility. He was a putty-gray being whose shape utterly defied all human standards. He seemed to possess a jelly-like body a protuberance for a head, in which there were two enormous hate-filled eyes. He stood in solid impassivity on mighty blocks of legs.

'Can you understand my tongue?' Vola demanded of him.

'I understand,' he responded, speaking purely by thought vibration, a being of immense scientific advancement. 'What would you have of me?'

'You are a beaten foe, my friend, and as such I demand information.'

'I shall not give it.'

'We have means of persuading you,' Vola warned him, and after a glance round the laboratory with his terrifying eyes he seemed to appreciate that she spoke the truth.

'What information do you wish?' he questioned. 'I am not prepared to give away scientific secrets. I will die first.'

'Your secrets are of no interest to me: we have no wish for conquest. I wish to know from which planet you come.'

'We call it Gorderiam, in the Ninth Inter-Galaxy.'

'Show me on the cosmic chart . . . '

Vola motioned to the gigantic scale drawn map of the Universe on the far wall. The prisoner moved to it on his mighty legs and considered it for a time, then he set a blunt one-fingered hand on a particular spot. 'There!' he said. 'Many light centuries from here.'

'But that is nearly on the outer rim of the Universe!' Vola cried in amazement. 'How long have you been travelling?'

There was no answer. Only the glare of the terrible eyes that revealed the cruel, mightily scientific brain behind them.

'Since you will not answer that, tell me why you attacked us.'

'Why not?' came the thoughts. 'Others have attacked you before us.'

'But why? We cannot fathom the reason. What can we ever have done to you? What is there on this world that you can seek when we are no higher in the scientific scale than yourselves?'

'We are escaping from the Black Terror. All of us are. Those nearest to it came first, fleeing from the Dark. When our world was threatened, we came, too. Others will follow. Your world is but a stopping place as we all flee onwards, away from the Black Terror.'

Vola looked puzzled. 'The Black Terror? What is that?'

'It is nothing, and yet it is everything. It is finality. It is death. It is the end of all things knowable. We have been fleeing from it for what must be endless generations of your time. To us, being of crystallized thought, distance is but a trivial barrier because we can cross space as fast as thought itself, inconceivably faster than light or your own magnetic force propulsion. Because we are crystallized thought we can destroy ourselves — as I do now!'

And with sudden overpowering force the creature's mind built up into a fiendish concentration. He literally wiped himself out with the power of his own thoughts and left behind only a haze of dispersing vapor.

'An amazing creature, Highness,' one of the scientists commented. 'Probably the ultimate of all evolution that ever will be — thought in a crystallized state. There was much we might have learned had he remained alive a little longer.'

Vola did not seem to be thinking of the

vanished intellectual giant. Instead she said:

'Have a space-machine prepared for me immediately. I must discover the meaning of this Black Terror if I possibly can.'

7

The Circle of Time

Soon, Vola was flying into the void with stupendous speed, and using the customary lines of magnetic force she reached a point finally where she could view the incredible maw of darkness, which was spreading inwards and devouring the stars and nebulae as it came. Even as she watched she saw certain of the distant stars waver and drown in the onrushing tide.

A tremendous sense of urgency gripped her, the certain knowledge that if something was not done quickly Hytro itself might be endangered. Yet the task of saving the planet from possible disaster was not hers: it was Cran Zalto's, as ruler.

Troubled, she returned home and thereafter spent an ineffectual period trying to arouse Cran from the lethargy into which induced emotions had plunged him.

He listened to all she had to say, studying her earnest face blearily — then at last he relaxed again without making any comment. Helpless, Vola sat gazing at him . . .

And Martin Clegg awoke with the resemblance of Cran Zalto in his mind. He had the feeling that somehow he and Cran Zalto were linked, that he was the being responsible for mental perturbations. But how to find out what it was all about?

There was Tom Cavendish, of course. He and Martin had been friends for a couple of years, being members of the same Discussion group — and Tom was a man with considerable scientific knowledge. In fact he had to have, to maintain his position as an electronic engineer.

Martin made a point of lunching in the Pyramid café that day, and as he had expected he discovered Tom in a far corner, munching away absently whilst he pored over a treatise. He looked up with a brief smile of welcome as he realized Martin had joined him.

'Where have you been putting yourself,

Mart?' he enquired. 'Haven't seen you for some weeks.'

'Oh — this and that.' Martin gave his order. 'And you'll probably see even less of me henceforth. I've — met a girl. I hope she might even be *the* girl.'

'Good man!' Tom smiled, and then with an effort dragged himself away from his treatise. 'Do I know her?'

'I don't think so. Elsie Barlow by name.'

Tom shook his head and then drank some coffee. He gave an encouraging look.

'You seek me out just to tell me that? Glad as I am to hear it, it isn't exactly an original happening, is it? I mean, men and women meet every day.'

'It's something else,' Martin said, pausing whilst the lunch was placed before him. 'I'm trying to decide whether I'm — ' He stopped, glancing towards the doorway as a girl came in and looked about her for a vacant table.

'There *is* Elsie now!' Martin exclaimed, getting up hastily. 'S'cuse me.'

He hurried across to her and she

smiled as she saw him coming. In another moment she was being introduced to the dour young man who had risen from the table.

'A great pleasure, Miss Barlow,' he assured her. 'Mart was just telling me about you.'

'Favourably, I hope?' the girl laughed, seating herself.

'Couldn't be more so!'

'Just how do you come to be here?' Martin asked in surprise, when the girl had stated her preference for lunch. 'Is it coincidence, or what?'

She shrugged. 'I often come in here because it's handy for the office.'

'Well, think of that! Maybe you and I have often looked right at each other and it never registered.'

Tom looked longingly towards his treatise then forced himself back to good manners. 'Er — Mart, what were you going to say when Miss Barlow arrived?' he asked. 'You were on the verge of — '

'Oh, it wasn't anything. Just some crazy notion I had.' Martin glanced back to the girl. 'Tom's an electronic scientist,' he explained. 'Tons of brains. Knows all about the Earth's history, too. Any scientific problems you have, bring them to Tom.'

'Mine are financial, not scientific,' Elsie smiled; then her smile faded a little as she saw the intensely thoughtful expression on Tom's face. 'Did I say something — out of place?' she asked uncomfortably.

'I wasn't listening, I'm afraid,' Tom responded. 'Excuse me looking at you so fixedly, Miss Barlow — '

'Do call me Elsie, please! I hate starchy formality.'

'Elsie, then. I was just thinking how much you resemble the ancient drawings of Queen Efrina.'

'Oh?' Elsie hesitated a moment and then ventured a cautious question. 'Was — was she attractive?'

'As near as ancient reconstructed drawings can make it, yes. The theory is that she was a queen of Atlantis long, long ago, before an unexplained catastrophe overwhelmed that city, and in fact the continent on which the city stood.'

'And where was it?'

'Approximately where the Atlantic is now. Near the Azores. Science believes that the Azores are the tops of the mountains which once ringed Atlantis.'

Elsie started on her lunch. 'I've heard of Atlantis, of course, but have never understood much about it. In fact I have always believed it to be a myth.'

'Anything but.' Tom shook his head solemnly. 'Certainly people *used* to think that, until the latest archeological discoveries showed otherwise. It probably contained one of the most scientific races ever to walk this planet. It was allied in some way with the Egyptian dynasty of that period — but whereas the Egyptians were dark-skinned and black haired, the people of Atlantis — the women anyway — were all golden haired and blue eyed. They had, however, a curious shape of ear and forehead, more marked in the higher social circles and particularly noticeable in the reconstructed prints and tablets referring to one Queen Efrina, who was obviously the highest woman in the land at the time of Atlantis' dissolution. You

179

have ears and forehead identical in shape.'

Elsie glanced at Martin and he shrugged. Then his eyes wandered to Tom.

'What are you trying to make out, Tom? That Elsie is a re-incarnated queen, or something?'

'If so I've certainly come down in the world,' Elsie commented. 'From queen to office girl in ten easy lives!'

'Joking apart,' Tom said, 'the resemblance is definitely there. I ought to know. The history of ancient civilizations is one of my favourite studies.'

'Dry old stick, isn't he?' Martin asked, grinning.

'Interesting, not dry,' Elsie corrected. 'Tell me, Tom. I'm a great believer in having lived before, you know, otherwise how does one explain that weird feeling — which everybody experiences sometimes — of having done this or that thing in identically the same way, under the identical situations, somewhere before? That might be a hangover from another life, mightn't it?'

'If so,' Martin said, 'it would suggest that life is repetitive, that everything moves in a circle.'

'I think it does,' Tom commented. 'Planets and suns are round; the Universe is round. Birth, maturity and decay all comprise one cycle. So life itself and Time may also be circular. We may only be living over again what has already been done endless times before.'

'We're drifting a long way from Atlantis and Queen Whatever-her-name-was,' Elsie commented; and Tom gave an apologetic smile.

'So we are! Well, as in the case of other lost civilizations, like those of the Incas, and so forth, there are records that have survived, and have been recently discovered. There is much to show that the Atlanteans had great scientific knowledge, and that they probably knew how to travel space. A reconstruction of events in forgotten ages seems to suggest that the Atlanteans escaped in a body into the void, before being overwhelmed by a cataclysm. What the cataclysm was nobody knows. It seems to have come some time after the Deluge, which was in an earlier part of Earth's history. They left behind odd bits and pieces, which were perhaps carried by floodwaters, and only found recently. Amongst these records were fine metal printings of Atlantean celebrities — and Queen Efrina, as I tell you, looked exactly like you.'

'Just coincidence,' Elsie said, thinking. 'If the entire race went into space she'd certainly go with them as a ruling dignitary — and presumably they never came back, according to history. So I couldn't look like her, could I? I mean, I couldn't possibly be a descendant of hers because nobody was left behind.'

'Of that I am not too sure,' Tom replied. 'I think that the land of Mu teemed with Atlanteans, and I do not believe that every one of them could escape into space. Some may have survived the disaster. Today there are probably hundreds of people who are descendants of the Atlanteans, but are not aware of it. With you the ancestry is decidedly marked. You are enough like the original Queen Efrina to pass as her.'

'Well, maybe she had a double,' Martin said, shrugging. 'I don't see it signifies very much in these hard times. I don't suppose I bear any resemblance to some ancient dignitary, do I?'

'Not many records of the Atlantean men seem to have survived, Mart, so I'm afraid I can't say.'

The sweet stage in the lunch had arrived and Atlantis went out with the greasy plates. The subject changed to commonplaces. Time and again Martin was on the verge of mentioning his own strange mental obsession, but checked himself each time — chiefly because of Elsie Barlow. His regard for the girl was such that he did not wish to have her thinking of him as an irresponsible young man without the power to direct his life correctly. She would never understand the mystery of a twinship. So he let the subject alone and parted from Elsie with the renewal of the promise to visit the cinema that evening.

And on Hytro, Cran Zalto was in the deepest depths of induced slumber. He dreamed so vividly that he seemed to live

— and a baffling sequence of events it appeared to be.

Part of the time he was seated at a desk drawing plans to scale and using such ancient tools of measurement as a protractor and set-square. There were many others about him in an airy office, and outside was the grey gloom of a provincial town lightened but little by the glow of a summer sun.

Then he was somewhere else — far out in space, inside a space-machine. A robot lay nearby and Vola was at his side. The robot, he knew, had a brain identical to his own, though its outward vestment was metal. But if ever the mind of that brain should take upon itself a fleshly form it would become *him*!

Strangely terrifying conception. And there was the Dark, yawning ahead of him without reason. Now he was travelling quintillions of miles. Now he was motionless.

He realized, in a sudden gleam of wisdom amidst the chaos that somewhere a Universe had been created. Upon its creation a lost image of himself had been shifted by cosmic forces across untold light centuries of space. Around the brain identical to his own there had formed a body. He was repeating himself, on a far distant world. He had duplicated Creation but given himself two bodies forever tied by a mental link. He had, by a process he could not understand, doomed all those who would come after him to the curse of dreams.

Vola, meanwhile, satisfied that the latest invasion had been smashed, was using all her scientific power to try and discover the nature of the Black Terror — and failing. She consulted the fifteen-brain robot, which was the Oracle of the planet, and it, too, found the explanation beyond it.

'The ruler sleeps and our world will be one day devoured,' Vola said bitterly, to the chief scientist of the laboratory. 'What is the answer to that one?'

'It is one which I hardly dare give, Highness. I would suggest the destruction of the sleep-inducing machines and removal of all robots.'

Vola reflected then she shook her head.

'No. That would bring endless trouble. Not only would my husband be involved, but all those of the retinue who have chosen sleep instead of action — '

'Highness — !'

At the urgent voice Vola turned. A messenger had just entered, his insignia proclaiming he was from the astronomical observatory.

'Highness, I have been asked to inform you at once that a further invading fleet appears to be on its way. As yet it is infinitely distant, at least seventeen kiastras, but all signs show that it is headed in this direction. What are my orders?'

'At the moment I have none,' Vola answered. 'I must endeavour to have the ruler speak. I am not really entitled to delegate for him.'

The man saluted and departed and a moment or two later Vola was back in the Hall of the Dreamers. The expression of profound content on her husband's face irritated her beyond measure. She controlled a very primitive urge to slap it and restore consciousness abruptly; then she thought better of it. She resorted to her usual formula — calling Cran by name, her tone leaving no doubt as to the urgency.

And Martin Clegg awoke with a violent start, his heart feeling as though it were going to burst through his ribs. For a moment or two he lay motionless and shivering in bed, then he began to calm again.

'Cran,' he muttered. 'I'm sure somebody called that name. But whoever heard of a name like that?'

Irritated, he switched on the bedside lamp. It was half-past two, about the most ungodly hour possible. Not that it was anything new to him to be awakened thus, for he had never had a peaceful night's sleep in all his life. The trouble was the business was getting worse. He was beginning to feel utterly swamped by something he could not understand.

All thought of sleep banished and the memory of an extraordinary name ringing in his brain he scrambled out of bed and began to dress wearily. By the time he had completed the task he was thoroughly awake.

'What's the answer?' he muttered to himself lounging to the window and looking out upon the sleeping city in the summer darkness. 'Am I one man alone in all the teeming millions who must be perpetually at the beck and call of something I don't understand? Is time a circle? Am I living something over again which I had thought dead and done with?'

With troubled eyes he looked out towards where the constellation Orion gleamed. Orion — fascinating, compelling, containing the key to his destiny, past, present, and future. Of this he was convinced. But then, at night, he was always possessed of these convictions. By day he wondered why he had thought on such things, when the unknown entity back of him was subdued by the power of his natural will.

'Sleeping tablets?' he asked himself. 'Yes, maybe they will help. I'll get some tomorrow.' And he did, but when he tried them the next night they had little effect on his outraged brain. He slept heavily, but his dreams were more violent and complex than ever. Three nights after he had become addicted to the tablets he visited the cinema with Elsie, and try though he would he could not concentrate on the film. In any case it was pretty ghastly stuff — the harrowing experience of a man accidentally sealed in a metal container and flung into a furnace. It seared an impression into Martin's brain, which just could not be eradicated, only in his dreams it took a different and even more terrifying form.

He was nothing more or less than a robot! Piece by piece he was being put together. He felt each agonizing twinge as metallic nerves were threaded up and joints were given the power of mobility. The queer thing was that he seemed to be looking at his designer who seemed to be thinking the very things that he was thinking. And behind the designer was Elsie Barlow dressed like a Grecian! Mad dream indeed.

Martin turned and cursed in his sleep. No, it was not Elsie Barlow. Just a girl who looked very much like her, who even had a similar figure. She was looking troubled, as though she did not in the least approve of what the man was doing. For a while there was a blessed respite, a brief quiescence, then Martin was disturbed again. This time he was inside some kind of vessel. It looked like a submarine, and the controls were very similar — No, not a submarine. Out there through the port there was a vision of endless stars, and a particularly 'half eaten' Milky Way.

'Now we shall see!' the creator said and Martin heard it quite distinctly even though he realized it was spoken in a strange language and that it was probably crossing endless gulfs of Time and Space.

Martin found himself lifted and lain flat in a smotheringly-small tube. As in all dreams he was weighted. He could not struggle. He could only endure anguish of mind — Then he was hurtling with stupendous velocity through space. On, and still on, at a speed defying computation.

Through the void and into darkness. Something within him seemed to click. He was disembodied, neither here nor there. He felt a compelling thought . . .

'The Universe is only a thought in the mind of a super-mathematician. You are the image of the mathematician! You are the image of the scientist who patterned you, in brain but not in body. Always, you will be the reflection of him, tied to him, endlessly, down the corridors of Time . . . '

'It's seven o'clock, Mr. Clegg!'

'Huh?' Martin asked thickly, pushing aside tangled blankets.

'Seven o'clock sir. Your regular morning call. Your cup of tea is outside.'

'Oh yes — thanks, Mrs. Pearson.'

Martin pulled himself up, rubbed his sweating face, and then scrambled out of bed. Outside it was warm and summery with a sun already high. He considered it dully.

'I am not as other men,' he decided, as he dragged on his shirt. 'I am only the image of the mathematician who created the Universe — ' He stopped and shook himself, 'What in blue hell am I talking about?' he demanded. 'How the devil *could* I be?'

Orion . . . Earth . . . Somewhere there was a connection, unless he was the connection. He was not sure if his dream had been a mad version of the film he had seen, flavoured by theories often expounded by Tom Cavendish — or whether he had really happened on some buried stream of memory which was striving to make clear to him the enigma of his life. He collected and drank his tea, then began shaving. Just for a moment, as he looked in the mirror to begin, he was stricken by an astounding thought.

Not only was he the brain image of a super-mathematician. He was the super-mathematician as well. A mighty scientist at the peak of evolution. He was born and yet was dead. He would be and yet had been. That which he was going to do he had already done.

'Hell,' he whispered, shutting his eyes for a moment. 'This is insanity! It must be old Uncle Ezra coming out in me.'

Old Uncle Ezra had been a chartered accountant, only his mania for figures had taken unexpected deviations and he had finished his life writing multiplication tables on the floor of an asylum cell.

'But it isn't that *kind* of craziness,' Martin insisted to his reflection. 'I'm normal enough in outlook, if it were not for these preposterous dreams ... I wonder why the devil did that woman in the dream look just like Elsie, except for her Grecian dress? Wonder how Elsie would look in a Grecian dress?'

He tried to picture the answer to his question, but his imagination was not powerful enough. He could hardly ask her to wear such an attire, even though it was summer — yet he felt that if she did it might solve a lot of things for him.

His chance came three days later when the firm for whom he was draughtsman gave a midsummer ball held in the grounds of the engineer owner of the firm.

Elsie could see no reason why she should not wear Grecian attire, and did so. Martin, through some kind of instinct he could not explain, dressed himself in a toga and shorts, adding arm and leg bands of imitation gold. Altogether he and Elsie made quite regal figures as they strolled out into the quieter byways of the grounds in the moonlight during a lull in the proceedings.

'Elsie, sit down a minute,' Martin said, taking her elbow. 'I want a word with you.'

They found a rustic seat and settled. The evening had *become* soft dusk, a mellow moon peeping through the trees. In the distance were the soft strains of a Strauss waltz.

'Yes, you're just like her,' Martin said at last, and Elsie glanced at him in surprise in the glow of the Chinese lanterns strung through the trees.

'Her? Whom? Or am I not the only girl in your life?'

'Only girl in *my* life, yes,' Martin answered ambiguously. 'I mean you're like somebody I've seen in my dreams recently. Absolute image of her.'

'Am I supposed to be flattered, or what? You're not making much sense, Mart.'

'No. I suppose I'm not,' he muttered, and hesitated on whether he should explain everything in detail. Then he changed his mind. The girl would never understand.

'I seem to have a lot in common with other women,' she remarked, after a pause. 'Not so long ago I was the image of Queen Somebody-or-other from Atlantis: now I'm like somebody you've seen in a dream. I don't know whether to be resentful or flattered.'

'I can understand you perhaps being a descendant of Atlantis, but how you come to be far out in space as well is a mystery.'

'What did you say?' Elsie gasped.

'Eh? Oh, nothing. Sorry. Just talking to myself. You know how dreams get on your nerves sometimes.'

'Not this badly!'

'Or maybe there are two,' Martin finished absently. 'Or maybe the Atlantean queen made a copy of herself and when she went out into space she happened to finish up in a far distant part of space and her successors lived in that far distant place. That would leave the copy and its descendants, of which you might be one.'

This time Elsie only gazed, her expression utterly blank.

'Sorry,' Martin apologized. 'Just rambling.'

'And the distance you cover!' Elsie whistled. 'For the love of heaven, Mart, whatever is the matter with you? I never heard a man talk so strangely before.'

'You forget Tom Cavendish,' he said dryly, and managed to change the direction of the conversation.

From then on he was more careful and did not allow his thoughts to find audible expression. The last thing he wanted was to upset Elsie or give her any clue that he was not, perhaps, quite as other men. She was obviously the kind of girl who liked all things normal, so it was just not worth the risk of upsetting her. If, and when, it came to a matter of marriage: well, to be straight, Martin realized he would have to explain. By then, though, he might have swung her so far on his side that he would take a chance.

Certainly Elsie did not realize that she, almost as much as Martin, was a creature of circumstance, a product of time and space. She had no clear memory stream that might have shown her that her first ancestor was a synthetic woman with an electronic brain, patterned after the image of Efrina of Atlantis. That incident was swallowed up in endless antiquity, and yet by the complexity of Time and Space it had yet to come. In the words of Ecclesiastes — 'That which hath been is now; that which is to come hath already been.' Perhaps he, like Martin Clegg, had glimpsed the underlying reality of the Universe and all things in it.

'It's getting chilly,' Elsie remarked, and hugged her bare shoulders with slim hands.

This put an abrupt end to speculations on Martin's part and they made their way to the terrace, and thence into the residence. It was three in the morning when Martin took his farewell of Elsie outside her home.

'Elsie, tell me something,' he said quietly, his expression hidden by the shadow of the trees around the gate and the high overhead moon. 'Are we just very good friends, or does it go deeper than that?'

She was silent for a moment, then she

said, 'I think it goes deeper than that, Mart. Now and again I keep having the oddest feeling — '

'Odd? In what way?'

'I suppose it's silly of me but now and again I have the notion that we have met before somewhere. Not only once, but many times — as though our lives have been interwoven, been part of some pattern. Or is it the moonlight?' Elsie broke off, her practicality coming to her rescue.

'It isn't the moonlight,' Martin assured her gently.

Silence. Then he realized she had kissed him and turned away.

'Same place, same time tomorrow,' she said, and unlatched the gate. 'Or rather today. It's not far from dawn.'

Martin watched her enter the house and close the door, then with his hands in his overcoat pockets he mooched through the streets back towards his own apartment house. As usual he went by way of Ridley's Common and gazed out towards Orion and the solitary splendour of Betelgeuse. He seemed extra bright tonight, winking with ruddy fire.

'The Universe was born because it was thought of by a master mind,' he murmured. 'And you, over the gulf of ages, united by bonds you can never fathom, are the master mind . . . You are not Martin Clegg; you are not Cran Zalto of Hytro in the constellation of Orion — You are an architect of worlds, and creator of yourself and all those patterned in your image, male and female.'

Martin hardly realized that he had been talking. It was as if the ghosts of memory winging across space had spoken for him. To even try and conceive what the words meant was supremely terrifying. That everything was his because he had made it. That everything would *be* his when he *did* make it — It was starting again. That crazy, insane circle of upended reasoning. The end before the beginning, and the beginning before the end.

Yet he had spoken of Cran Zalto. Who was he and what was he? Was he the . . . Somebody?

Yes, Cran Zalto was the Somebody. On faraway Hytro he was emerging from slumber for a while. He found the Hall of Dreamers quiet in the Hytronian night, but there was the soft glow of the subdued lamps and the movement of the robots, as gentle and feathery as gossamer . . . They began to massage him with thistledown lightness. His cushions were rearranged; cooling perfumes were sprayed in a fine mist upon his magnificent body. He raised himself on his elbow and thought. The impressions of his dreams were still upon him, clear and distinct as he had allowed his mind to wander through depthless space.

'Perhaps I have found the answer,' he whispered. 'I am one person, and a being called Martin Clegg on a far distant world of lowly development is the Other. In the past I created him in robot form and at the dawn of a new Universe his brain, patterned after mine, began to function and, by the laws of chemistry and creation, took on a fleshly form. But cosmic currents decreed that he should mature light-centuries away from me, yet with his mind always linked to mine because we think alike, absorbing the same thought frequencies. We shall always be together in mind, unless one of us dies.'

'Should that happen,' Cran mused, 'there will come, for one of us, cessation of worry concerning the other. But the mind of the dead one being free, it will be drawn instantly to the possessor of the *other* mind, and link with it. The gulf will be destroyed and either he, or I, will become possessed of the complete mind and be troubled no more.'

Cran relaxed, a little overwhelmed by the conception he had experienced — and it was already fading. It had only emerged briefly, clear-cut from the realm of mental absolutism in which he had been drifting. For the first time he knew the explanation for the Other. Only if the Other's body should die, and unity of minds could take place, would he assume his true personality. Or would he? Would he be part Cran and part Martin Clegg? Or, even, would the mind of Clegg, less drugged by induced dreams, take complete possession? Cran did not know. He was feeling sleepy again —

Then he jerked upright, startled. 'In the *past*, I created him?' he repeated blankly. 'When? I never did any such thing! Yet, if I didn't, how did he come into being?'

Complexity. Enigma. The inscrutable forces of the Universe making mockery of Cran's sleep-deadened brain. He relaxed again, beaten, and the robots cared for him as he drifted away into the depthless realms where only dreams, and sometimes the dreams of Reality, held sway . . .

And in her own suite, the suite which should have been shared by her husband had he been anything like natural, Vola tried to sleep and could not. Being a normal woman she worked hard by daylight and slept only to refresh herself, but this night slumber would not come. She was thinking of an invading fleet remotely visible in the telescopes, heading in this direction. She was thinking of Cran and his eternal somnolence. And she wondered why she was perhaps the only woman in the royal retinue who behaved like a worker, who disdained all the comforts of induced emotions and preferred instead to try and improve perfection.

As it was denied to Elsie Barlow of Earth, so a vivid memory was denied to Vola of Hytro, identical to her sister light centuries away. The weavings of Time and distance had brought Efrina here to Hytro and Vola was her direct descendant, with all the fire and spirit that had possessed her progenitor. Vola was not aware that her ancestor had created a double, and since it had only been physical and not a mental double it had no link to disturb, annoy, and even distract. This much Vola was spared. To her there was no such person as Elsie Barlow, just as to Elsie there was no Vola. Their minds never once worked in sympathy. So neither knew the tortures of the damned which science gone mad had inflicted on two men who were compelled by natural law to think of each other, in each other, and about each other.

To Vola there was only granted supreme bafflement at the behavior of her husband. She felt slighted, hurt, and bitterly resented that she was not only ignored as a wife but also had the entire responsibility of the planet on her shoulders as well. She was not aware that Cran retreated into dreams to try and gain solace from mental perturbation: she imagined, as well she might, that she was the cause of the trouble.

So on this night, for the first time in her life, Vola began to cry — and, like a child, she cried herself to sleep . . .

★   ★   ★

The following day Martin's thoughts were not on his work, and because of it he made mistakes, which, in a plan drawn by a draughtsman, was a fatal thing to do. So he had to spend a couple of hours beyond his ordinary time clearing up the mess. The main reason for his distraction of thought was not so much Cran this time, as Elsie.

He kept thinking of the previous night when he and Elsie had, for a brief while, stepped out of ordinary civilized life and become part of another age and existence. Or at least that was what it had felt like — and the more he pondered it, and remembered Elsie's assertion that she had met him before, the more he believed it. Somewhere — way back — it had happened, but the exact detail was lost in time.

It was a summons from the boss, also working late in his own office, which broke up Martin's speculations. He entered the great man's abode and did not feel particularly sanguine at the grim expression on that dogged face.

'How long have you been with us, Clegg?' the chief asked.

'Er — quite a time, sir.' Martin was remembering that on the previous night the boss had been roaming around dressed as Nero and the memory was somewhat disconcerting.

'Of late, Clegg, I haven't liked your work.' The chief sat back in his chair and reflected, the diagonal light from the desk lamp casting over his powerful features. 'Three times recently the department manager has handed me plans, which have your initials, and in each case they have been hopelessly wrong.'

'I'm sorry, sir,' Martin apologized.

'I don't doubt it — but being sorry isn't enough. This is a firm of engineers, Clegg, and when machines are built to faulty specifications all kinds of unpredictable things can happen ... I don't want to be hard on you because all of us have little worries that upset our judgment — but I do think you ought to explain. When you first came to us your work was excellent. I had high hopes for you. I even considered you as undermanager in the department ... Naturally, I cannot do that any more. What *is* it, Clegg? You don't appear to be ill, and you certainly know your job when you exert yourself. So, what's holding you up?'

Martin was silent, thinking of something, somebody, very far away, as hazy as a nebula on the rim of infinity.

'Girl trouble?' the boss suggested, with a friendly grin. 'I've been young myself, you know, and there's nothing like a woman for putting you off balance. I remember when I was about twenty-two I — ' The boss cleared his throat and changed position 'Never mind! We're

206

discussing you: not me. I want to help you, Clegg, because I like young people. I know you have no parents so maybe you'd like to confide, eh?'

Still Martin hesitated, not because he did not believe in the chiefs statement but because —

'I'm troubled by being two people, sir,' Martin said suddenly.

'Eh?' The boss was prepared for almost anything, but certainly not for this. His bushy eyebrows shot up.

'That's my trouble,' Martin went on. 'And what makes it worse is: if I explain myself it sounds even more silly. I don't suppose you have ever been haunted by the belief that you are living two lives at once.'

'You mean — a *double* life?' the chief asked doubtfully.

'Not in the accepted sense, sir. I don't mean two women pushed away in separate corners. I mean that *I* am two people. Half the time I live here, on this planet, as a perfectly ordinary draughtsman with a very charming girlfriend — who I hope will marry me later. The rest of the time, especially when I'm asleep, I am on a far distant world.'

The chief was gazing with his grey eyes wide open, like a hairy baby waiting for its bottle.

'Because I'm partly somebody else it becomes very difficult to concentrate,' Martin added lamely.

'Yes, I can imagine. Excuse me, Clegg, but what the devil are you *talking* about?'

Martin shrugged. 'As I said, sir, it sounds ridiculous.'

'That is an understatement. Er — in what other way does this remarkable delusion affect you?'

'It isn't a delusion, sir: I've had it too long for that. Ever since I can remember, and it is steadily becoming much more dominant. There are times when I am not sure whether I am Martin Clegg or Cran Zalto.'

'Whom?'

'You wouldn't understand, sir. But you asked for an explanation, and I'm giving it. I know it sounds fantastic, and I am probably the only man in the world who lives two lives so thoroughly and makes a complete mess of both of them.'

'Quite frankly, Clegg, I am not

concerned with your two lives. It is my blueprints that matter. You'll have to do better. Much better.'

'I will try, sir. After all, I ought to be able to handle a few blueprints when I am actually the man who created the universe.'

The chief rose to his feet. Coming round the desk, he put a hand on Martin's shoulder.

'My boy, I'd say take a long rest in a quiet spot — if I could spare you. But I cannot. So in between times, when you are not here, you'd better give yourself all the mental relief you can. You are overstrained.'

Martin only smiled — rather sadly.

'And I shall look forward to an improvement,' the chief finished. 'In the old days you would probably have been fired on the spot — but trained men aren't that easy to get these days, not in the technical field, anyway. So we'll forget your mistakes up to now and have things right from here on. That right?'

'I hope so, sir,' Martin responded, and with that left the office.

But he knew perfectly well that there

never would be an improvement. There couldn't be as long as that unknown remained to dominate his life. In fact, the puzzle was: where was it all going to *end*? This perpetual drifting would have to cease some day, or else it was going to lead down, down, down, into God knew what . . .

And, just as he had anticipated, Martin did *not* improve. He went on making mistakes, but in many instances he succeeded in rectifying them before they were noticed. His perpetual struggle with himself and the Other, however, was commencing to leave its mark upon him. As the summer moved on into autumn, he became much more morose. Elsie Barlow, to whom he had become engaged, could not help but notice it — but for a long time she held her counsel, thinking that perhaps Martin was tired from overwork.

And still he did not give her the facts, nor did he intend to until the matter of marriage came up definitely for decision,

The progress of time was also evident in the far reaches of the Universe, infinitely beyond Orion and the planet

Hytro. It affected an armada approaching from the furthest depths of the Universe and watched by the scientists of Hytro with untiring vigilance. Because of the incomprehensible immensity of space the armada seemed to move but little in the passing weeks, whereas actually it must have been travelling at many thousands of miles to the second.

Vola was the most worried being on the planet. She had ceased her efforts to try and arouse Cran — at least for the time being — and was devoting her energies to checking the defenses. Eventually a desperate battle would have to be fought — and whether it would be won or not depended on how scientific were the invaders. Vola was not fool enough to think that Hytro's scientific power could win every time. One day there would come invaders who were infinitely cleverer, and that would be the end. The fact remained that Cran was the real man to deal with the situation, and Vola felt his absence keenly.

Not that he himself was troubled. He lay fast asleep with the robots around

211

him. He was not living in space but on a far away world where a woman who resembled Vola was his only interest. The most curious thing about her was her name — Elsie Barlow. And why she should be an inhabitant of such a backward planet was a mystery.

By some fluke or other Martin was still a draughtsman; with the same firm, though he had the instinctive feeling it could not last much longer. What made it particularly difficult was that Elsie was not a believer in long engagements and was already hinting that they ought to be getting married.

'Oh sure, we certainly must,' Martin agreed, as they strolled home together one evening in the early winter.

'But, Mart, that's all you ever say,' Elsie objected. 'And then you don't do any more about it. Is there something wrong?'

'No. Not particularly.' Martin was moodily silent for a moment. 'Just that I wish I could feel more sure of my job. I don't seem to be making out so well.'

'You're probably over-anxious. Can't be anything more. And we can't go on walking about forever, can we?'

'No — course we can't,' Martin agreed; but even then he did not commit himself any further.

He just did not dare. When he decided on marriage he had to admit everything else and thereby lay an intense human problem. Elsie might stay beside him — but she might just as easily walk out of his life and leave him to the complete domination of this Other being so far away.

More weeks passed. Invaders moved closer to far away Hytro. Cran still slept amidst his cushions. Vola still tried to tighten up every defensive measure. On Earth it was the week before Christmas and Martin realized that he could hold out no longer against the girl. He just had to explain.

'What is the *matter* with you?' she demanded, as they paused in the act of window-gazing for Christmas.

'Am I talking to myself?' Elsie demanded, as Martin did not answer. Then as he gazed at her absently: 'Remember me? I'm the girl who came out with you on a shopping tour. You might as well be a corpse.'

'There may be more in that than you realize,' Martin said, musing.

'Mart, what's wrong?' Elsie took his arm. 'Why do you behave so strangely these days? Are you ill, or something?'

'No, I'm not ill. Never felt better — physically.'

Martin realized he said a good deal more, but all of it seemed to be an exact repetition of something he had said before an infinitely long time ago — and yet it was also something he would say again, far in the future. For the first time in his life he was appreciating the fact that past, present, and future are all in one circle, repeating — endlessly.

When he next became really conscious of himself he was out on Ridley's Common, with Elsie looking at him uncertainly. She spoke, half in fear. Martin looked at her in surprise.

'What's the matter?' he asked. 'You sound scared.'

'I — I hardly know how I sound, Mart. You're acting so strangely . . . '

Yes, he had been here before, said these words before. And so had Elsie. There

214

was something crushingly inescapable about it all. But he had an explanation to give, and he gave it. Deliberately, knowing it was no use holding back any longer. It seemed pitifully commonplace when Elsie asked:

'Have — have you seen a psychiatrist? He could probably make you straight.'

The psychiatrist? Yes, of course. He had been in the scheme of things before, too. And so had Tom Cavendish. Sure enough the evening finished with Tom Cavendish, and he held forth on the scientific explanation — as far as he could trace it — of Martin's trouble. Martin felt he could anticipate every word, so clear was the memory of it having been enacted before.

Out in the street, on the way home again, Elsie did not hold back her opinion.

'Scientists are fatheads! Ask them a straightforward question and they come out with all manner of high-sounding words. As if you could have a twin up in the stars there! I never heard of anything so crazy!'

At her words something boiled up within Martin. Here was this perfectly ordinary girl daring to besmirch the name of a scientist with her silly prattle, and directing it at him — he who had created a Universe, who *would* create a Universe, who —

'Sometimes, Elsie,' Martin said, 'I think you have a very tiny mind. You're a decent girl, but you — '

'Tiny mind, did you say?' Elsie came to a stop, her lips pouting in the light of the street lamps.

'You must have, otherwise you'd see Tom's explanation is the only possible one!'

'I don't know which is the crazier — you or Tom!' Elsie snapped. 'But I do know I'm not going to walk around with you and be insulted! What sort of fun do you think I'm having? — going out with a man who looks half asleep and explains it by pointing at the stars? I know lots of chaps who can give me a good time, and the sooner I tell them so, the better!'

'Elsie — wait a minute — '

Martin made a grab at her arm and missed. He sighed and remained where he was, watching her slender figure heading away under the street lamps, her heels clicking purposefully. When at last she had vanished from view round the corner which led to her home avenue he pressed finger and thumb wearily to his eyes.

'Maybe she's right,' he muttered. 'I can't be much of a pal to walk out with.'

He began moving again, mooching along with hands thrust deep in his overcoat pockets. By the time he had reached his rooms he had come to a decision. He locked the door of his little combined apartment and, quite deliberately, went to the small table and began to write a letter. When he had finished he read it through . . .

*December 21*st.
To Whom it May Concern,

I, Martin Clegg, have decided for various reasons to take my own life, and I absolutely absolve anybody else from possible blame. I find my life purposeless — and rendered more so by the attitude of my former fiancée, Elsie Barlow, though I can easily understand — and forgive — her impressions of me. I also feel that by dying I may release another person, far away, from the chains that are holding me . . .

Martin paused in his writing and reflected. He knew that the words he had just penned were incorrect. By dying he would probably become part of that distant being who had always had such a claim on him. Well, what did it matter anyway? Nobody would understand him, in any case. He began to finish the letter . . .

One man may understand — Tom Cavendish. In any case, the world will not miss a not-too-good draughtsman.
Martin Clegg.

Martin nodded to himself, put the letter in an envelope, and then addressed it to his landlady. This done he crossed to the cupboard and took from it the bottle of sleeping tablets which, his nights always being disturbed, he had taken to using for some months past.

He shook several into his palm,

considered, and then added several more. Without even troubling to remove his coat or shoes he put the tablets on his tongue, washed them down with water, and then lay on the bed.

He smiled a little as he yawned and drowsiness began to assail him. Though the single light in the room was still on he could see fairly well through the un-curtained window. The stars were out there, gleaming frostily. Far away was the constellation of Orion.

Orion . . . Orion . . . His thoughts began to become woolly and his limbs seemed to have enormous weights on them. There was dim confusion in his ears that grew to a drowning roar of sound —

Then he was moving, light as thistle-down. He seemed to have no body. He was hurtling through space, many times faster than the speed of light, infinitely faster than any rocket projectile could ever travel. Outwards, ever outwards, where everything was soundless and stars and suns winked with blinding intensity in the airlessness of space.

Orion . . . It was no longer a constellation.

He had come too close to it for that. He could see planets, seven worlds swinging round mighty, ruddy Betelgeuse, worlds so far away from Earth that no telescope had ever glimpsed them. How could they when even their parent sun, Betelgeuse, appeared no larger than a pinpoint?

But now Betelgeuse was a magnificent sun, his colour varying constantly between deep red and brilliant orange. Here was a sun with a diameter of 300-million miles, and with a bulk of 40-million times more than Earth's own sun. A monarch of the void indeed.

Martin felt himself moving, down towards the world third in order from Betelgeuse. He caught a glimpse of landscape bathed in that fantastic orange glare. There were majestic cities, pale blue oceans, clouds here and there. Mountains, plains, forests — everything a mature planet could possess . . .

It was dark.

THE END

CLIMATE INCORPORATED
THE FIVE MATCHBOXES
EXCEPT FOR ONE THING
BLACK MARIA, M.A.
ONE STEP TOO FAR
THE THIRTY-FIRST OF JUNE
THE FROZEN LIMIT
ONE REMAINED SEATED
THE MURDERED SCHOOLGIRL
SECRET OF THE RING
OTHER EYES WATCHING
I SPY . . .
FOOL'S PARADISE
DON'T TOUCH ME
THE FOURTH DOOR
THE SPIKED BOY
THE SLITHERERS
MAN OF TWO WORLDS
THE ATLANTIC TUNNEL
THE EMPTY COFFINS
LIQUID DEATH
PATTERN OF MURDER
NEBULA
THE LIE-DESTROYER
PRISONER OF TIME

We do hope that you have enjoyed reading this large print book.

Did you know that all of our titles are available for purchase?

We publish a wide range of high quality large print books including:
Romances, Mysteries, Classics
General Fiction
Non Fiction and Westerns

Special interest titles available in large print are:
The Little Oxford Dictionary
Music Book, Song Book
Hymn Book, Service Book

Also available from us courtesy of Oxford University Press:
Young Readers' Dictionary
(large print edition)
Young Readers' Thesaurus
(large print edition)

For further information or a free brochure, please contact us at:
Ulverscroft Large Print Books Ltd.,
The Green, Bradgate Road, Anstey,
Leicester, LE7 7FU, England.
Tel: (00 44) **0116 236 4325**
Fax: (00 44) **0116 234 0205**

THE VANISHING MAN

Sydney J. Bounds

Popular novelist and secret agent Alec Black is on an undercover mission on Mars. The Martian colonists are preparing for a major offensive against earth and someone is stirring up war-fever. Black must try to prevent it, or the whole system will be engulfed in atomic war. When Black finds himself shadowed by a man who, when confronted, vanishes into thin air, his investigation turns into his strangest case and very soon he's plunged into a dimension of horror . . .

TOYMAN

E. C. Tubb

Space-wanderer Earl Dumarest is on the planet Toy, hoping he'll get information on the whereabouts of Earth, his lost home world. But nothing is given freely there and he must fight in the Toy Games to gain the information he needs. He's forced to be like a tin soldier in a vast nursery with a spoiled child in command — but there's nothing playful about the Games on Toy. Everything is only too real: pain, wounds, blood — and death . . .